Blaze

Do you need a cowboy fix?

New York Times bestselling author
Vicki Lewis Thompson is back with more...

Sons of Chance

*Chance isn't just the last name of these rugged
Wyoming cowboys—it's their motto, too!*

Saddle up with:

SHOULD'VE BEEN A COWBOY
(June 2011)

COWBOY UP
(July 2011)

COWBOYS LIKE US
(August 2011)

Take a chance...on a Chance!

Blaze

Dear Reader,

When I was in college, my dad happened to be the Dean of Students, which created a massive problem for any guy who wanted to date me. Most boyfriends are a little nervous dealing with a girl's father, but if that father has the power to destroy an entire college career, the stakes go way up.

I gave top cowhand Clay Whitaker a similar problem. He has a major attraction to the only daughter of Emmett Sterling, foreman of the Last Chance Ranch in the Jackson Hole area of Wyoming. As a former foster kid, Clay cherishes the ranch as his last chance for a real home. The family treats him as one of their own, and Emmett is the father he's never had. Getting cozy with Emmett's daughter Emily has the potential to ruin everything.

Yet Clay's a hot-blooded cowboy with a taste for risk. Something tells me he will go for it, despite the high stakes. I fell in love with this guy, as I do all my heroes, but he has a special place in my heart because he started with so little and has so much to lose. Well, and he also looks amazing in a pair of jeans....

Welcome back to the Sons of Chance series! It should be illegal to have this much fun!

Forever yours in cowboy country,

Vicki Lewis Thompson

Vicki Lewis Thompson

COWBOY UP

TORONTO NEW YORK LONDON
AMSTERDAM PARIS SYDNEY HAMBURG
STOCKHOLM ATHENS TOKYO MILAN MADRID
PRAGUE WARSAW BUDAPEST AUCKLAND

Recycling programs
for this product may
not exist in your area.

ISBN-13: 978-0-373-79628-1

COWBOY UP

Copyright © 2011 by Vicki Lewis Thompson

ABOUT THE AUTHOR

New York Times bestseller Vicki Lewis Thompson's love affair with cowboys started with *The Lone Ranger*, continued through *Maverick* and took a turn south of the border with *Zorro*. She views cowboys as the Western version of knights in shining armor—rugged men who value honor, honesty and hard work. Fortunately for her, she lives in the Arizona desert, where broad-shouldered, lean-hipped cowboys abound. Blessed with such an abundance of inspiration, she only hopes that she can do them justice. Visit her website at www.vickilewisthompson.com.

Books by Vicki Lewis Thompson

HARLEQUIN BLAZE
544—WANTED!*
550—AMBUSHED!*
556—CLAIMED!*
618—SHOULD'VE BEEN A COWBOY*

*Sons of Chance

To get the inside scoop on Harlequin Blaze and its talented writers, be sure to check out blazeauthors.com.

Don't miss any of our special offers. Write to us at the following address for information on our newest releases.

Harlequin Reader Service
U.S.: 3010 Walden Ave., P.O. Box 1325, Buffalo, NY 14269
Canadian: P.O. Box 609, Fort Erie, Ont. L2A 5X3

Prologue

Jackson Hole, Wyoming July 21, 1961

CARRYING HIS COFFEE MUG, Archie Chance joined his wife, Nelsie, for their evening ritual of rocking on the front porch, gazing at the mountains and discussing… whatever came up.

Archie settled in his chair and took a sip of his coffee before broaching the subject on his mind. "What do you think about frozen semen?"

Although some women might have been taken aback by such a question, Nelsie didn't bat an eye. "Are you fixing to freeze yours?"

That made him laugh. How he loved this woman. "Nope. Don't think there would be much call for my semen considering that I've only been able to produce one son in all these years."

"That's because you go for quality and not quantity."

Archie gave her a smile. Their son, Jonathan, now fifteen, had turned out pretty damned well, if Archie did say so. The boy lived and breathed ranching just as Archie had hoped he would. There was no question that Jonathan would take over the Last Chance when the time came.

"So whose frozen semen are you interested in, then?" Nelsie asked.

"Goliath's. I've been reading about folks shipping frozen bull semen all over God's creation and making money doing it. Seeing as how the Last Chance is still a cattle operation and Goliath fetches a hefty stud fee, I wondered if I should look into it."

Nelsie's rocker creaked softly as she appeared to ponder that idea. "Goliath might not take to having his semen collected."

"I know."

"I would imagine he prefers to impregnate cows the old-fashioned way."

"Too bad. It's the sixties. Times are changing. Goliath needs to change with them."

Nelsie turned to gaze at him. "And you need more money to get this horse venture off the ground."

"Yeah." He cradled his mug in both hands and watched the fading light play across the flanks of the Grand Tetons. "It's a hell of a lot more expensive than I thought it would be, Nelsie, and it may take years, but someday the Last Chance is going to be known for raising the finest paints in Wyoming."

1

July, present day

THE STALLION'S SCREAM of sexual frustration ricocheted off the walls of a shed that smelled like fresh lumber and honest sweat, both human and horse. The Last Chance Ranch baked under a sun that shone with uncharacteristic ferocity. Clay Whitaker, who'd recently been put in charge of the ranch's stud program, wiped his face on his sleeve.

The new shed could use an air-conditioning unit—humans would appreciate it, at least. The horses probably wouldn't care, judging from the ardor of Bandit, the black-and-white paint that claimed a higher stud fee than any other stallion in the Last Chance Ranch.

Despite the heat, Bandit seemed desperate to mount the mare contained in a small pen only a few feet away. He would never get the chance. The pretty little chocolate-and-white paint named Cookie Dough was a decoy.

Instead of mating the old-fashioned way, Bandit

would have to make do with a padded dummy so that Clay could collect the semen, freeze it and ship it to a customer in Texas. Shipping frozen horse semen promised to add an increased revenue stream to the ranch operation, or so Clay projected it would.

Nick Chance, middle son of the family that operated the ranch, was on hand to help. A large-animal vet, Nick, co-owned the Last Chance along with his older brother, Jack, his younger brother, Gabe, and their mother, Sarah. Clay had known all of them for ten years.

Theoretically, sperm collection was a simple task. Nick would keep a firm grip on Bandit's lead rope as the stallion mounted the dummy, and Clay would move in with a collection tube. Instead, Bandit seemed determined to get to the mare, and both men's yoked Western shirts were stained dark with sweat.

Nick glanced around the small shed. "We need to get us some air-conditioning in here."

"That's exactly what I—" The rest of Clay's response was drowned out by another scream from Bandit, right before he did exactly as he was supposed to and mounted the dummy. Grasping the tube, a twenty-five-pound piece of equipment designed to keep the semen at an even temperature, Clay moved in for the crucial part of the operation.

When Bandit was finished, both men stood back to let the stallion rest on the dummy for a moment.

Nick glanced over at Clay. "Shall I offer him a cigarette?"

"Very funny."

"I invited Jack to watch, but he declined."

"I'm not surprised." In fact, Clay would have been amazed if Jack had shown up for Bandit's session. Jack didn't much like the idea of collecting and shipping frozen semen, but he recognized times had changed and had agreed to let Clay put his animal science degree to good use.

Still, Bandit was Jack's horse, and Jack thought the collection process was completely undignified. Maybe so, but Jack couldn't argue with the income it would generate. Being in charge of this new operation meant Clay had an important job at the ranch he loved so dearly, but it also allowed him to give something back to the only real family he'd ever had.

Orphaned at three, he'd been shuffled through a series of foster homes until turning eighteen. Then he'd come to work at the Last Chance, where Sarah and her husband, Jonathan, had treated him more like one of their sons than a hired hand. But he'd formed the strongest bond with Emmett Sterling, ranch foreman and the closest thing to a father Clay had ever had. Emmett had recognized that Clay had a brain, and encouraged him to save for college.

Working while he attended school had meant taking six years to complete a four-year program, but now he was back. Jonathan Chance's death from a truck rollover almost two years ago had shocked Clay and made him even more determined to use his education to benefit the family.

Bandit slowly lifted his head as if he'd recovered enough to dismount from the dummy.

"Guess we're about done here," Nick said. "I'll take him back to his stall and then get Cookie Dough."

"Thanks." Clay hoisted the canister to his shoulder and left the shed. On his way to the tractor barn and the incubator he'd set up there, he had to pass by the horse barn, and he glanced around uneasily.

Emmett's daughter, Emily, had arrived late last night so she could help celebrate her dad's sixtieth birthday tomorrow. Her white BMW convertible—sporting a California vanity plate that read SURFS UP—sat in the circular drive, top down and tan leather upholstery exposed to the sun. Well, that fit the impression Clay had of her—spoiled and irresponsible.

He'd met her at her father's fiftieth birthday, soon after he'd come to work at the ranch; but Clay hadn't seen her since. She might have visited while he was away at college, though she'd made it obvious ranch life didn't suit her.

Emmett had sent her large chunks of his paycheck every month when she was a minor, so the guy was always broke. After she came of age, everyone expected Emmett to have more money. He didn't, and eventually it had come out that he was still writing sizable checks to his daughter.

Although Clay would never say so to Emmett, he—along with most everyone at the ranch—resented the hell out of the ungrateful little leech. When he'd first met Emily, he'd done what any normal eighteen-year-old guy would do when confronted with a gorgeous blonde. He'd flirted with her.

She'd said in no uncertain terms that cowboys weren't

her style. The rejection had stung, but her disdain for cowboys in general had to be even more hurtful to her father. Clay had vowed to forget her hot little body and continue about his business.

Unfortunately the image of her Daisy Dukes and low-cut blouses had stuck with him, no matter how often he'd tried to erase the memory. He could still close his eyes and see her prancing around like she was in some beauty pageant. With any luck she'd packed on some pounds in the past ten years and wouldn't look like that anymore. With any luck, he wouldn't have direct contact with her at all.

So much for luck. Here she came, long blond hair swinging as she walked out of the horse barn with Emmett.

Clay swallowed. Sure enough, she'd put on a few pounds—in all the right places. Her black scoop-necked T-shirt had some designer name across the front and, to Clay's way of thinking, the designer should've paid Emily for the display space.

Her Daisy Dukes had been replaced by cuffed white shorts that showed off a spectacular tan. She'd propped oversize sunglasses on her head and now she pulled them down over her eyes as she glanced in his direction.

Clay had no trouble picturing her wearing a bikini and sipping an umbrella drink while she lounged by the pool in her hometown of Santa Barbara. He imagined her smoothing coconut-scented suntan oil over every inch of that gorgeous…

Whoa. He'd better shut down that video right quick. No way was he lusting after Emily Sterling. That was a mistake on so many levels. For one thing, he didn't even *like* her, and he prided himself on only getting involved with likable women.

Emmett looked at him and nodded in approval. "Looks like you got 'er done."

"We did." Clay dredged up a polite smile as he drew closer. "I'm glad your daughter arrived okay." He made out the letters on the front of her shirt. BÉBÉ, with an accent mark over the last *E*. Probably French for *babe*. Appropriate.

"She showed up about eleven last night," Emmett said. "I never thought I'd be grateful for cell phones, but I sure am when she's on the road. Emily, do you remember Clay Whitaker?"

"She probably doesn't." Clay adjusted the collection tube, that was getting heavier by the second. "That was a long time ago. Anyway, nice to see you again, Emily. If you'll excuse me, I need to—"

"Do what?" She motioned to the metal tube balanced on his shoulder and grinned. "That thing looks like a rocket launcher."

"Um, it's not. Listen, I really have to—"

"At least tell me what it is, then."

"Semen collector," Emmett said helpfully.

"Really?" Emily took off her sunglasses and peered at the tube. "So did you collect some semen just now?"

"Yes, and I need to get it into the incubator."

"And then what?"

"Oh, it's a whole process," Emmett said. "Clay studied how to do it when he was in college, and now the

Last Chance can ship frozen semen all over the country. All over the world, if we want."

"Flying semen." A ripple in her voice and a glitter in her green eyes suggested she was trying not to laugh. "What a concept. That canister is pretty big. Is there that much of it?"

Dear God. Clay couldn't have come up with a worse topic of conversation if he'd tried all day. "Not really. There's insulation material, and…and…"

"The AV," Emmett said.

"What's an AV?"

Of course she'd ask.

"It's an artificial va—" Emmett stopped and coughed, as if he'd finally realized this really wasn't a fit subject to be discussing with his daughter, who hadn't been raised on a ranch and wouldn't be used to a matter-of-fact discussion of female anatomy.

Clay stepped into the breach. "Artificial vacuum," he said. "It's an artificial vacuum."

"Huh." Emily's brow furrowed. "I'm not sure I understand. Something's either a vacuum or it's not."

Emmett put his arm around her shoulders. "It's complicated. And very technical. Anyway, we need to let Clay get on with his job."

"Right." Emily flashed her even, white teeth and winked at him before replacing her sunglasses. "I don't want spoiled semen on my conscience. See you later, Clay."

"You bet, Emily." He headed off, cursing under his breath and trying to ignore his gut response to that smile. If he didn't know better, he'd classify that wink as flirting; but that couldn't be right. She'd told him once that she was a city girl who had no intention of getting mixed up with a shit-kicking cowboy, and he wasn't about to make the same mistake twice. The perception that she'd flirted with him just now was only wishful thinking on his part.

Stupid thinking, too. How could he have sexual feelings for a woman who continued to bleed her hardworking father for money while sneering at that good man's lifestyle? A woman like that shouldn't interest Clay in the least and definitely shouldn't stir his animal instincts. Ah, but she did. Damn it, she did.

Maybe she presented a challenge to his male ego and all he really wanted to do was take her down a peg. He was far more confident around women now than he had been ten years ago, and he realized that they found him attractive. Could be he'd like to prove to Miss Emily that a shit-kicking cowboy could ring her chimes better than any city boy.

He wouldn't follow up on that urge, though. Emmett had been like family. The guy was his idol. That meant Clay wasn't going to mess with Emily. End of story.

"CLAY WHITAKER SEEMS to have turned out okay." Emily congratulated herself on sounding vaguely interested, when inside a wild woman shouted *Take me, you bad boy! Take me, now!*

She watched Clay walk across the open area between the horse barn and the tractor barn. A girl could get used to that view—tight buns in faded jeans and shoulders broad enough to easily support a large canister of horse semen. Horse semen, of all things!

She was dying to know how that process worked. Biology had been her favorite subject in high school, but her mother, a buyer for Chico's, had steered her into fashion design. Unfortunately, she had no talent for it.

Collecting horse semen—now that would be interesting. Apparently it was a sweaty job. The back of Clay's shirt clung to his sexy torso and the dark hair curling from under his hat made him look as if he'd stuck his head beneath a faucet. The guy was hot in more ways than one, and pheromones had been coming off him in waves.

He must have had those same deep brown eyes when he was eighteen; but, if so, they hadn't registered with her. Today was a different story. Looking into his gorgeous eyes had produced an effect on her libido that was off the Richter scale. Either Clay had acquired a boatload of sexual chemistry over the years, or she'd been a stupid seventeen-year-old who hadn't recognized his potential.

She wondered if she'd been rude to him back then. At the time she'd been full of herself and full of her mother's prejudices against cowboys. If she had been rude, she hoped he'd forgotten it by now. He probably had, after not seeing her for so long.

"Clay's developed into a top hand." Emmett studied her as if trying to guess what was going on in her head.

"That's good to hear." She didn't want him to figure out what she was thinking, either. "I know you're fond of him." In fact, she'd been a little jealous over the years when he'd bragged about Clay, although she'd never admit that to her dad. On the other hand, knowing Emmett had Clay had eased her conscience about not visiting more often.

"He's a good guy," Emmett said. "So, do you still want that coffee?"

"What? Oh, right! Yes. Absolutely." At home she'd developed a midmorning Starbucks habit, something she'd confessed to Emmett during their tour of the barn when she realized she was running low on energy. But the encounter with Clay had boosted her spirits without the benefit of caffeine. Still, coffee was always welcome. She fell into step beside her father as they continued on to the house.

"I don't know if I told you that Clay got his degree in animal science this spring."

"I don't think you mentioned that." She knew he wasn't comparing Clay to her, but still, she'd dropped out of college because she couldn't see wasting the money when she didn't know what she wanted to study.

Her mother kept pushing retail, preferably involving fashion. Emily's heart wasn't in it, and finally she'd told her mother so. She'd briefly considered marine biology and had volunteered in the field, but that hadn't felt quite right.

Her current receptionist job couldn't be called a career decision, either. She sighed. "When I see somebody like Clay, who has his act together, I feel like a slacker."

Emmett shook his head. "Don't be too hard on

yourself. Some people take longer than others to figure out what they want to do."

"Maybe so, but Clay's had so many obstacles to overcome…"

"We all have obstacles."

"I suppose, but you told me he spent his childhood going from one foster home to the next. That's major trauma."

"You haven't had a bed of roses, either, what with no father around."

"That wasn't your fault, Dad." She hated that he still felt guilty about the divorce, nearly twenty-five years after the fact. Before she'd been old enough to think for herself, she'd accepted her mother's assessment that Emmett was to blame for the divorce. Gradually she'd come to see that it had been a bad match that was doomed from the start.

"It was partly my fault," Emmett said. "First off I let your mother take you to California, and then I only came over to visit two or three times."

"Yes, but Santa Barbara isn't your kind of place." They'd reached the steps going up to the porch and her dad's boots hit the wood with a solid sound she'd missed hearing. She'd missed other things, too, like the way his gray hair curled a little at the nape of his neck, and how his face creased in a smile and his blue eyes grew warm and crinkly with love when he looked at her.

She hadn't always appreciated how handsome he was because she'd been so influenced by her mother's assessment of cowboys as unsophisticated hicks who went around with a piece of straw clenched in their teeth. Her dad did that sometimes, but he also moved with fluid grace, and he was as lean and muscled as a man half his age.

He blew out a breath, which made his mustache flutter a bit. "Doesn't matter if it's my kind of place or not. I should've visited more often." He paused with one hand on the brass doorknob. "I'm sorry for that, Emily. More sorry than I can say."

"It's okay." Bracing her hands on his warm shoulder, she rose on tiptoe and leaned in under the brim of his hat to give him a kiss on the cheek. "I've always known you love me."

"More than anything." His voice was rough with emotion. "Which is why we both need to get some coffee in us before we turn into blubbering fools and embarrass ourselves."

"And a Sterling never turns into a blubbering fool."

"That's exactly right." Clearing his throat, Emmett opened the door and ushered her inside.

Although the main house didn't have air conditioning, the thick log walls kept the rooms cool even in the heat of summer. The second story helped, too. Emily adored the winding staircase that, according to her dad, had been expertly crafted more than thirty years ago by the Chance boys' grandpa Archie.

Emmett had told her that Archie had been a master carpenter who'd designed every aspect of this massive home for both beauty and practicality. Even Emily's mother, who pretty much despised anything to do with ranching, had once confessed that she found the house to be spectacular.

A huge rock fireplace dominated the living room, and although no fire burned there, the scent of cedar smoke had worked its way into the brown leather armchairs and sofa gathered in front of the hearth. No doubt the large Navajo rugs hanging on the walls had absorbed the smell of the fire, too. Its woodsy fragrance combined with that of lemon oil furniture polish would always be connected in Emily's mind to the Last Chance.

She'd assumed salt air and ocean waves were her favorite backdrop; but walking into this living room late last night had felt a bit like coming home. Because her dad's little cabin was small, Emily stayed upstairs in the main house when she visited. She hadn't thought she was particularly attached to the place, but last night she'd realized that wasn't true. She loved it here.

Her dad caught her looking around the living room. "Maybe if I'd provided your mother with a house like this," he began, "then she—"

"She still wouldn't have been happy. Face it, Dad. She isn't content unless she's living by the ocean near some really good shopping."

"I discovered that too late."

"So did she." And Jeri had never remarried, which told Emily that her mother had loved her dad and probably still did. Although Emma might be the feminine version of the name Emmett, Emily was darned close. "She married you without stopping to think that she finds horses and dogs exceedingly smelly."

Emmett laughed. "And she's right, they are. But I happen to love that about them."

"Believe it or not, I kind of do, too."

He thumbed back his hat to look at her. "I had a feeling you did."

"All along I've pretended that taking barn tours and riding was a drag, but the truth is, I've always looked forward to being around the animals."

"You'd better not let your mother hear you say that."

"I know. I suppose I thought it would be disloyal to her if I said I liked them." She gazed at him for several seconds. All her life she'd been told that ranching was nothing but dust, horse poop and endless drudgery. Because of that she'd told herself her visits were only an obligation to maintain a connection with her father.

She'd let three years go by since the last time, and she might not have made the trip this summer except that her father was turning sixty. To her surprise, she was really glad to be here. And she'd finally admitted to her dad that barns and horses appealed to her.

In fact, she had the urge to spend more time hanging out at the barn and getting to know the horses. Of course, that could have something to do with Clay Whitaker. Clearly if she wanted to see more of Clay she'd need to become involved with the animals he tended.

She turned toward her father. "Do you think we could take a ride this afternoon?"

"I might be able to work that out. I need to pick up some supplies today, and maybe we could stretch that into a little shopping trip in Jackson." He brightened. "I could ask Pam to come along so you could meet her. You two could shop while I warm a bench outside."

"That sounds great, Dad." Actually, it didn't. He'd told her last night about Pam Mulholland, who owned the Bunk & Grub, a bed-and-breakfast inn down the road. It seemed her father had a girlfriend, and Emily wasn't sure how she felt about that. "But I meant a horseback ride."

"Oh. I'm afraid that's not in the cards for today, sweetheart. I really do have to run several errands and I'm not sure how long they'll take. Sure you don't want to come along?"

She couldn't blame him for thinking she'd love to go shopping. Three years ago she'd been all about buying stuff, partly because she'd known it would please her mother if she came back with clothes. "It's funny, but now that I'm here, I feel like staying put," she said. "Maybe I'll just take a walk around the ranch this afternoon." *And see what Clay's up to.*

"A walk?"

She smiled at his puzzled expression. "I know. Cowboys don't walk, but I do."

Emmett looked down at her feet. "Then you'll need to put something on besides those sandals."

"I packed the boots and jeans I bought when we went shopping in Jackson last time I visited."

"You still have those?"

"They're like new. I felt like a fake wearing them in Santa Barbara. I'll probably feel like a fake wearing them here, but I want to give it a shot."

"Okay." He gave her a look that was pure protective dad. "Promise me you won't try to go riding by yourself."

"I promise." Years ago she would have resented the implication that she couldn't handle riding alone. But she hadn't been on a horse in three years, and she was old enough now to appreciate his warning as a gesture of love. "I know my limits. I can ride a surfboard like nobody's business, but I don't have much practice on a horse." She paused. "Maybe one of the hands could go with me."

"That's an idea. I could send Watkins."

She remembered Watkins as a shortish, older guy with a handlebar mustache. Nice enough, but not the person she had in mind.

"No, not Watkins," her dad said. "He has a toothache and would spend the whole ride talking about it."

"Then how about—"

"I could send Jeb, but…I don't know. That boy gets distracted by a pretty face. I'd ask one of the Chances, but Nick's scheduled to worm our little herd of cattle, Gabe's off at a cutting horse event, and Jack's taking Josie to the obstetrician today." He glanced at Emily. "I did tell you that Josie's pregnant?"

"Yes. You gave me the rundown last night, and I think I have it all straight. Josie and Jack are expecting their first. Gabe and Morgan have little Sarah Bianca, who's one month old. Nick and Dominique are waiting a bit before having kids."

"Right. Okay, let me think. There must be somebody I would trust to take you."

She did her level best to sound indifferent. "I don't suppose Clay could go."

"Hey, that's a great idea! I don't know why I didn't think of it. I'll ask him."

Bingo.

2

FOR THE FIRST TIME SINCE he'd come to live at the Last
Chance, Clay dreaded lunch hour. Years ago, before
Clay had come to the ranch, Archie had begun a tradi-
tion of gathering everyone in the main house at midday
so that news could be exchanged and plans made. In
fact, when the east wing had been added, Sarah had
suggested creating a large lunchroom because the family
dining room had become too crowded.

The new space held four round tables that each sat
eight, and windows on the north and east provided light
and spectacular mountain views. Hands ate in the bunkhouse for breakfast and dinner, rotating the cooking
chores among themselves, but they considered lunch a
treat, both for the setting and the food. Sarah insisted
on tablecloths and cloth napkins because she believed
in adding a little class. The guys tolerated that because
Mary Lou Simms, the family's cook, always put on a
mouthwatering spread.

Mary Lou's cooking was one of the many things
Clay had missed while he was in Cheyenne going to

school. Today's menu featured fried chicken, potato salad, corn on the cob and biscuits, all served family style. The heaping platters and bowls coming out of the kitchen smelled as good as they looked, and normally Clay would have been licking his chops.

Instead, he was on Emily Alert. She'd be here, sure as the world, and he wanted to stay as far away from her as possible. He hesitated just inside the doorway and scanned the room, which was already filling up.

"Just the man I want to talk to."

He recognized Emmett's deep voice as the foreman gripped his shoulder from behind. Clay turned, knowing that Emmett wouldn't be walking into the lunchroom alone. As expected, Emily stood beside him, and to Clay's surprise, she seemed unsure of herself.

Even more surprising was her outfit. She still wore the scoop-necked T-shirt with BEBÉ splashed across the front, but she'd traded the shorts for a pair of jeans that looked as if they'd never seen the light of day, and tooled boots with nary a scuff mark on them. Clay found it hard to believe that she'd decided to dress like the locals so she could fit in better, but that's exactly what her change of clothes appeared to suggest.

"Let's find us a place to sit," Emmett said.

Clay stifled a groan. Trapped. He'd considered skipping lunch completely, but he was starving and he hadn't come up with a decent excuse for staying away. Traditions had taken on new significance since Jonathan's death, and the hands made every effort to be there at noon each weekday.

Nick and his wife, Dominique, a tall woman with her

glossy brown hair cut short, sat at a table with Sarah. Emmett ushered Emily in that direction, and Clay had no choice but to follow.

Nick stood as Emily approached. The Chance boys, thanks to a firm hand from Sarah, had the manners of diplomats. Sarah's mother, Lucy, had been an NYC runway model, and Sarah had inherited her mother's classic beauty and carriage. Although she was in her mid-sixties and her sleek bob was silver, she could pass for a woman fifteen years younger.

Sarah had taken over Clay's education in the social graces, too, and he was grateful. She gave a slight nod of approval as Clay helped Emily into a chair and introduced her to Dominique, who hadn't been part of the ranch the last time Emily visited.

Finally he sat down, and there was Emily, right beside him, giving off a fragrance that reminded him of sun and salty air. He'd only seen the ocean once, during a brief vacation taken by one of his foster families. On that trip he'd noticed lots of girls who looked like Emily, blond and wearing skimpy clothes to show off their tans. She was exotic, and he was unfortunately, drawn to that.

He'd hoped to escape sitting at the same table with her, and now here they were knee-to-knee and thigh-to-thigh. If Clay had thought he could get away with it, he would have scooted his chair closer to Sarah, on his other side. But that would look too obvious, so he worked on not making body contact.

No one else sat at their table for eight. Once the food had been passed and everyone had started to eat, Sarah glanced over at Emily with a friendly smile. "You look like you're getting serious about this ranch visit. I don't think I've ever seen you in jeans and boots."

"Nope, you haven't." Emily put down her drumstick. "I bought these a while ago, but this is their first outing. I'm hoping I'll be able to go riding this afternoon."

"The problem is, I have errands to run," Emmett said, "so I thought maybe Clay could take Emily out for an hour or so." He bit into a fried chicken breast.

Yikes. This was getting worse by the minute. Fortunately, Clay had an excuse. He quickly chewed and swallowed a forkful of potato salad. "I'd be glad to, but I have plans for this afternoon."

"Collecting more semen?" As Emily picked up her drumstick again and looked at him, she had a definite gleam in her eye. "I find that fascinating. I'd love to watch."

Damn it, she *was* flirting. Well, it wouldn't get her anywhere. "Sorry, but that's not on the schedule. I have another job I need to do." He buttered his ear of corn and sent a pointed glance in Sarah's direction. She'd deliberately created some errands for Emmett to run today because they needed him gone for a few hours so they could start setting up for tomorrow night's party.

Emmett expected a party, of course. But Sarah had decided to surprise him by switching the venue from the Spirits and Spurs—Josie's bar in the nearby small town of Shoshone—to an old-fashioned cowboy cookout where they'd all ride in on horseback. Clay thought Emmett would love that, so he'd volunteered to truck the tables, benches and firewood out there and build a fire pit.

"That's true, you do have chores this afternoon," Sarah said. "But you might be able to work in a ride after they're done."

"Maybe I could help with the chores," Emily said.

No. That's all he needed, to be stuck alone with her on party detail.

"That's a great idea," Sarah said. "Then he'll be done that much faster. I would take you out riding myself, Emily, but I've got a list a mile long."

Emmett split open a steaming biscuit and piled butter on it. "And it's all to do with my sixtieth, I'll bet. I keep telling you folks not to make a fuss over this."

"We're not making a fuss," Nick said. "We'll all head to the Spirits and Spurs tomorrow night like we usually do for special occasions. We'll have some drinks and a meal. Somebody's liable to drag out a birthday cake, but that's about the extent of the fuss."

"It better be. And no presents. Is that understood?"

"Too late, Dad," Emily said. "I hauled presents all the way from Santa Barbara, and you're gonna open them or else."

His expression softened. "Sure, sweetheart. I'll make an exception for you, but nobody else had better be showing up with packages."

"I can't guarantee that won't happen." Nick put down a corn cob and reached for another. "But I can guarantee that some of them will be gag gifts, so you might as well resign yourself to the process, Emmett. The hands deserve to have their fun at your expense."

The foreman sighed and raised his eyes to the ceiling. "Good thing these decade birthdays don't come more often." Then he turned his attention to Dominique. "And I suppose you'll be taking pictures."

She paused, her fork in midair, to give him a sweet smile. "Don't I always?"

"Yes, and they're fine pictures, mostly because I'm not in them. So take pictures of everybody else if you want, but the world doesn't need a record of me opening up a box with a whoopee cushion inside or blowing out a bunch of candles. And I sure as heck don't want to see my mug hanging with your other work in that gallery in Jackson."

Emily laid a hand on his arm. "The world might not need a record of you holding a whoopee cushion and blowing out candles, but I do." She glanced over at Dominique. "Please take a gazillion pictures of my dad during his party, okay?"

Dominique gave Emily a thumbs-up. "You've got it."

Clay listened with interest. Emily didn't sound like a spoiled brat who was only interested in the money she could squeeze out of her dad. Instead she sounded like a daughter who dearly loved her father and looked forward to celebrating his birthday.

She might be putting on an act for the benefit of those sitting at the table, though. As far as he knew, she was still accepting monthly checks from this man even though she was certainly old enough to earn her own living. Still, Emmett obviously basked in Emily's affection. Clay hadn't realized until now how much the guy adored his only child.

That kind of parental devotion used to set off a wave of longing in Clay, but these days he was more philosophical about being an orphan. After all, he'd been taken in by the Chance family. He might have started off life at a disadvantage, but he'd wound up pretty good.

And although Emmett wasn't technically his father, the guy filled that role in everything that mattered. He'd latched on to Clay from the get-go and always had his back. Emmett seemed to recognize that Clay needed an advocate. But maybe Emmett had needed Clay, too, as a stand-in for his absent daughter.

So now Emmett was asking Clay to take Emily riding. That was a gesture of trust, no doubt about it. Sarah's suggestion that Emily help him with party chores was a decent idea, too.

He could be gracious and take her with him out to the meadow. She could carry the benches and find rocks for the fire pit. It wasn't so much to ask that he include her after all the support Emmett had given him over the years.

He turned to Emily. "I'd appreciate it if you'd help me with the chores I have, and then we should be able to take a short ride later this afternoon."

Her answering smile dazzled him more than it should. "I would love that. Thank you, Clay."

"You're welcome." He looked away before she could see the effect she had on him. Heat shot through his body and settled in his groin. The rush of sexual awareness left him so shaky that he dared not pick up his fork or his water glass in case somebody noticed how he was trembling.

Good God, he wasn't some inexperienced teenager anymore. In the time since he and Emily had first met he'd had two serious girlfriends and several who would've liked to become serious. These days he knew his way around a bedroom and understood a thing or two about pleasing a woman once he got her in there.

And yet, one brilliant smile from this California girl had reduced him to the hormonal kid he'd been ten years ago. She hadn't wanted him then, but he had a strong suspicion she wanted him now. He wasn't sure why, because she sure as hell wasn't interested in sticking around Jackson Hole, and he was here for the duration.

Curiosity, maybe. She'd never indulged herself with somebody like him and had decided now was as good a time as any.

But none of that mattered, because no matter what she had in mind, nothing would happen between them. Emmett's trust guaranteed that. Clay would sooner cut off his right arm than betray the man who'd encouraged him to be the person he was today.

EMILY WASN'T SURE HOW she managed to eat anything at all as the meal progressed, and several times she almost dumped food on herself. Sitting next to Clay was like surfing in a storm—exhilarating but dangerous. He'd showered and changed before coming to lunch, and she almost wished he hadn't. His pine-scented cologne was nice, but she preferred the raw energy of his sweat-soaked body.

She wasn't sure who was generating the most sexual heat as they sat side by side eating lunch, but she sensed that he was as turned on by her as she was by him. He was nervous about that, though, and she didn't blame him. He clearly idolized her father, and anyone with half a brain would be able to tell that Clay was a principled guy. He wouldn't want to do anything that would upset Emmett.

She didn't want to upset Emmett, either, so her fascination with Clay was a tricky business. As much as her dad wouldn't want Clay seducing her, conversely he wouldn't want her seducing Clay, especially if she didn't have any intention of sticking around. And she didn't.

Maybe on this visit she liked the ranch better than she had before, but that only meant she considered it a good vacation spot. There was really nothing for her to do here. She didn't possess the particular skill set that would make her a...what had her dad called Clay? A top hand.

No, she was a far cry from being a top hand. She still hadn't figured out what she was good at. She loved to surf, but not enough to make a pro career out of it. Fashion design was out, and retail sales bored her to tears.

But she wouldn't solve her career dilemma hanging around the Last Chance. Once her visit was over, she'd return to her receptionist position at a medical complex in Santa Barbara. Maybe she'd go out with the cute doctor who kept asking her for a date. She hadn't been seriously involved with anyone since last year, when a surfing buddy had proposed.

She'd realized he was far more emotionally invested than she was and had gently turned him down. Besides, she had no business marrying someone when she didn't know where her life was headed. She wished she could be more focused, like Clay. Spending time with him this afternoon might give her some insights. At the very least, she'd be able to enjoy the sexual buzz they had going on.

As the meal ended and everybody stood to leave, Clay helped her from her chair—a gallant gesture she wasn't used to from the men she knew. "Thanks." She turned to him. "Do you have a cell phone?"

"Yes. Why?"

"I thought you could call me when you're ready for me to help you."

He grinned. "How about if I just come up to the house and get you?"

Oooh. Great smile. She curled her toes into the leather soles of her boots. "That works."

Emmett put an arm around her shoulders and kissed her on the forehead. "If you go riding later on, see if somebody will loan you a hat."

She glanced up at him. "Why do I need one?"

"For the most part, to keep you from being sunburned."

"Dad, I surf every weekend, and nobody wears a hat while they're on a surfboard. I have a good base tan and I have sunglasses. That's enough."

Her father looked over at Clay. "Would you see that

she puts on a hat before she goes out? I know we have extras lying around somewhere."

"Excuse me." Emily inserted herself between the two men. "I will not be treated like an obstinate female who needs to be managed by the men who know more than she does."

Clay laughed. "Then don't be obstinate. Wear a hat."

"Why should I?" She was intrigued by the fact that he was joking with her instead of getting irritated. She liked that kind of easygoing attitude.

"Because you're at a higher altitude here than you're used to, so the ozone layer's thinner and you could still burn. Besides that, if you're going to help me this afternoon, you're going to sweat, and the hat will keep the sweat from running in your eyes. I suppose you could wear a do-rag, instead, but personally I think the hat would look better on you."

Well, then. She hadn't thought about the value of a hat as an accessory. She should have, after being conditioned in that direction for most of her twenty-seven years by her fashion-conscious mother. If Clay thought she'd look better in a hat, no further argument was needed.

She turned to Sarah, who had been standing to one side watching the action with obvious amusement. "Got a hat I might be able to borrow?"

Sarah nodded. "Come with me."

3

EMMETT GLANCED AT CLAY. "Look, I hope she won't be in your way this afternoon. I didn't ask what you had on your agenda."

And Clay wasn't at liberty to discuss that. "It'll be fine." He would make it so, regardless of his strong attraction to the golden California girl.

"I invited her to come with me so she could do some shopping—my treat, of course. To my surprise, she wanted to stay here, instead."

"Huh." That surprised Clay, too.

"I know. I thought she loved to shop. Three years ago when she came to the ranch, we made a couple of trips into Shoshone, but the stores there aren't what she's used to. So when I took her back to the airport, we built in extra time for her to browse through those fancy places in Jackson."

"She was here three years ago, then. I wondered how often she'd made it over."

Emmett looked sad. "Not often enough, but I can't blame her for that. It works both ways. Like I told her this morning, I could have made more trips to Santa Barbara."

"Yeah, but…" Clay thought of the freeways and the traffic snarls and grimaced.

"I don't relish that area, either. But until this time, I didn't think she relished staying on the ranch—yet she comes to see me, even so."

"What do you mean *until this time?*"

Emmett rubbed the back of his neck. "I took her on a tour of the barn, like always. In the past, she acted like that was no big deal. I could tell she liked the horses, but she wouldn't let herself really get into it. I figured her mother had brainwashed her pretty damned well. But this morning was different. Apparently she's starting to think for herself."

"That's great." Clay hoped the foreman wasn't making too much of a passing fancy on Emily's part. He didn't want the guy to get his hopes up that Emily would suddenly turn into a cowgirl.

"I know what you're thinking, son."

Clay's chest tightened with emotion. He loved having Emmett call him *son*, even though he knew that cowboys used that word loosely and Emmett probably didn't mean it in a literal sense. "I'm not thinking anything, Emmett," he said.

"Sure you are. You're thinking that I'm an old fool who imagines his daughter is going to magically fall in love with ranching."

Clay sighed. "You're not an old fool, but it would be only natural if you—"

"Don't worry. I made that mistake with her mother.

I knew California was where Jeri wanted to be, but I thought I could convince her otherwise."

Something in Emmett's expression told Clay that those wounds had never healed. That might be another reason Emmett hadn't taken many trips to see Emily. He would have had to see his ex, too, which would have been painful if he was still in love with her.

Clay thought he might be and wondered if Pam Mulholland had any inkling of that. The two had been dating for more than a year without making a commitment. Emmett said that was because Pam had way more money than he did, but that might not be the whole story.

By now the dining room was empty except for Clay, Emmett and Watson, who had recently started helping Mary Lou clear the dishes in exchange for extra dessert.

Mary Lou bustled over, her gray hair in disarray as usual and her cheeks pink from working in a warm kitchen. "Did you two get enough to eat? I'm about to serve Watson an extra piece of cherry pie, and you're welcome to have a second serving if you want one."

Emmett patted his flat stomach. "Thanks, Mary Lou, but I couldn't fit in another bite. You outdid yourself again."

"Thanks, Emmett." She beamed at the praise. "I do love my job. How about you, Clay? More pie?"

"It's tempting, but no thanks."

"All right, then." She began stacking the dessert plates from each place setting at their table.

Watkins came out of the kitchen and headed toward them. "Hey, quit doing my job, Lou-Lou."

Her cheeks turned a shade pinker. "Then speed it up there, Watkins. We need to get this place clean."

"We will, we will. Leave those for me and go cut me a nice big piece of your delicious pie. And put some ice cream on top." The stocky cowboy winked at her as he reached for the dishes in her hand.

"Oh, for heaven's sake. If you insist." She handed over the dishes and walked back toward the kitchen.

Instead of stacking plates, Watkins gazed after her. "What a woman."

Clay watched in fascination. He'd thought something might be going on between Watkins and Mary Lou, but he hadn't been sure until now. "Are you sweet on her, Watkins?"

Watkins nodded, which made his handlebar mustache twitch. "Have been for years. Once I tried to get her to marry me, but she claims she's never marrying anybody. So I backed off, but lately…let's just say I might be making progress."

Emmett clapped him on the shoulder. "Clearing dishes and complimenting her on her cooking just might get the job done. Not that I'm an expert on women. What's your opinion, Clay?"

Clay held up both hands. "Don't ask me about women. They're a mystery."

"Ain't that the truth." Watkins glanced toward the kitchen. "Well, my pie should be about ready. Catch you later, boys."

After he left, Clay looked at Emmett and raised his eyebrows.

Emmett shrugged. "He's been carrying a torch for a long time," he said in a low voice. "You may not believe it, but she used to be a real babe."

"You know, I can believe it. And I've always loved her spunky attitude. I—" He stopped talking when Emily walked into the room. Talk about a babe. The snug T-shirt and form-fitting jeans would make any guy take a second look, but Clay had a thing about women in cowboy hats.

This one was tan straw, a warm-weather alternative to felt. The brim curved downward in both the front and back so it partly shielded her eyes in a sexy, flirty way. The more Emily adopted a Western style, the more Clay liked what he saw.

"How's this?" she asked as she came toward them.

Clay dialed back his response several notches. "It'll do."

"Good choice." Emmett's weathered face glowed with pride. "Fits nice."

Sarah appeared and crossed to where they were standing. "Looks good, huh? Fortunately we wear the same size."

"Sarah said I could keep this," Emily said. "But that seems silly if I'm only going to wear it while I'm here."

Some of the glow faded from Emmett's expression, and Clay ached for him.

No matter what Emmett had said about not expecting too much, it was obvious he'd allowed himself to hope that Emily wouldn't abandon her newfound interest in the ranch once she left. He nodded. "Guess so. Wouldn't want to let a good hat end up in the back of a closet. Well, I'd better get going if I intend to finish up those errands in town."

"Oh, that reminds me." Sarah pulled a slip of paper from the pocket of her jeans. "Here are a few more things I need while you're there. Also, Pam called and asked if you'd stop by the Bunk & Grub, and I'd really appreciate it if you'd look in on my mother and make sure she remembers about the party tomorrow night."

Emmett looked over the list. Then he trained that piercing blue gaze on Sarah in a manner Clay knew well. It meant that Emmett suspected something was going on and he intended to find out what. "You wouldn't be stacking up the errands to keep me away from the ranch all afternoon because of some scheme or other, would you now, Sarah?"

"Goodness, no! Why would I do a thing like that?"

"Because I've known you for thirty-some years, and you look like you're up to something. I'm warning you, if I come back from town and a passel of folks jump out of the bushes yelling 'surprise,' I will be one unhappy cowhand."

Sarah patted his arm. "I promise that won't be happening. Besides, your birthday's tomorrow."

"Which means the only way you could surprise me is to stage the party tonight. I wouldn't put it past you, either."

"You are so suspicious." Sarah gave him a big smile.

"You will love your birthday party, Emmett, and it will take place on your birthday, not the night before."

"Time will tell if you're putting me on or not. Anyway, I'll see you folks later, and there had better not be any shenanigans taking place while I'm gone." Settling his hat on his head, he left the dining room.

Sarah studied the beamed ceiling of the dining room and twiddled her thumbs as his footsteps receded down the hall leading to the living room. Only after the front door had opened and closed did she drop her gaze to Clay's and burst out laughing. "He's *such* a baby when it comes to birthdays."

"He knows something's going on," Clay said.

"What is it?" Emily looked eagerly from one to the other. "*Are* you going to surprise him tonight?"

"No." Sarah glanced over at the door to the dining room as if worried that Emmett might have crept back down the hall. "Emily, go make sure he's left."

"Be right back." Emily hurried out of the dining room.

Sarah moved closer to Clay. "He really will love this cookout. But if he knew about it in advance, he'd pitch a fit because we're going to extra trouble on his behalf."

"You're right, he would."

"But it's going to be so perfect. I realized this morning that you'll need to dig two fire pits, one for the bonfire and one we can let burn down to coals for grilling the steaks."

"I can do that."

Emily came back in, her face pink with excitement. "He's really gone. So what are you planning?"

"Clay can explain it all. I need to go check with Watkins, if he's still in the kitchen. His guitar was missing a string and I need to make sure he's fixed it."

"He's still there," Clay said, "but you might want to knock before you go in."

"I *see*." Sarah grinned. "Thanks for the warning. Catch you two later. Call if you run into any glitches." Then she walked toward the kitchen. "Sarah Chance is on the move!" she called out. "If there's anything going on you don't want me to see, you'd better cease and desist immediately!"

Emily looked at Clay. "What the heck is that all about?"

"Just a little romance between Watkins and Mary Lou. Come on. We have tables and benches to load into the back of a pickup."

"Okay." She fell into step beside him as they headed down the hall lined with windows on the right and family pictures on the left. "This visit is turning out to be way more interesting than I expected."

That patronizing remark set his teeth on edge. Added to her comment about not needing the hat once she went home to California, he decided to broach the subject of her attitude. "You know, this ranch may not be your favorite place in the world, but could you pretend it is, for your dad's sake?"

She stopped in her tracks. "Wow. You are definitely hostile."

He spun to face her. "I suppose I am. I love that man like a father, and you—"

"I love him like a father, too. *My* father, in fact."

He wondered for the first time if she resented all the attention Emmett had devoted to him. "Point taken."

She gave him a brief nod, as if at least that much was settled. "Anyway, I don't want to give any impression that I might like to live in Wyoming. To me, that would be crueler than being honest about my feelings. My mother gave him that kind of false hope, and I think he's still hurting because of it."

Clay hated to admit it, but she made sense. He wished she loved ranching the way Emmett did, but if she didn't, pretending could possibly do more damage. He took a deep breath. "You're probably right. I apologize. I have no business sticking my nose in, anyway."

"Sure you do. You love him. And from the way he raves about you and your accomplishments, I think he loves you, too."

"He raves?"

"Oh, yes. He brags about the way you carefully saved your money for tuition and then worked odd jobs while you took classes in Cheyenne. He was so proud of your grade point average. And when you got that scholarship, he mentioned it to me several times."

Clay gazed at her as his understanding grew. "It's a wonder you don't hate my guts."

"At times I did, although I don't like admitting that. Besides, he was born to be a dad, and I haven't given him much chance at that. Knowing you were here relieved my feelings of guilt."

"Still, I'll bet you got tired of hearing about my accomplishments."

She shrugged. "It's hardly your fault that I'm not

focused like you and can't for the life of me figure out a career. My dad's not likely to brag about my surfing ability, so that leaves him with nothing to boast about when it comes to his only child."

"Do you have a job?"

"Of course I have a job. How do you think I support myself?"

He decided not to mention that he'd been convinced she didn't support herself, that she was living off the money Emmett sent her every month. She might not appreciate knowing that most everyone at the Last Chance knew he sent checks and wondered why when he was no longer financially obligated. They all assumed Emily was living on that money, or at the very least, only working part-time to supplement his generosity.

But her finances and her job situation were absolutely none of his business. "I'm sorry," he said. "I was out of line starting this conversation in the first place, and we have a lot of work to do before your dad comes home. We should get going." He started back down the hall.

"Going where?" She lengthened her strides to keep up with him. "You still haven't told me the plan."

Briefly he outlined the details. He wondered if she'd find it hokey, but she responded with enthusiasm.

"That sounds like so much fun! Sometimes we have bonfires on the beach and cookouts, too. Usually somebody brings a docking station for their iPod instead of having live music, but a guitar player sounds terrific. Will there be dancing?"

"That's an excellent question. Knowing the Chance family, there should be dancing."

"Yay! I love to dance. I…just realized that I have no idea if my dad dances or not. I should know that, shouldn't I?"

"Not if you've never been around when dancing was part of the program." He reached the front door and opened it for her.

"Thanks." She tossed her hair back over her shoulder and smiled at him. "I'm enjoying all the gallantry around here."

"Sarah insists on it, and besides, it's the cowboy way to show respect toward a woman." He stepped onto the porch and closed the door behind him. That's when he looked out at the circular drive and noticed her convertible, top still down, leather upholstery exposed to the sun.

He couldn't stand it. "Do you have your car keys with you?"

"No, but I can get them. Is my car in the way?"

"You can leave it there, but you need to put the top up. You'll ruin the leather seats."

"It's stuck."

He glanced over at her. "Permanently?"

"I don't know. I pulled over at a rest stop around eight last night and decided to put the top down for the rest of the way, so I'd be sure and stay awake. When I got here, it wouldn't go back up. I meant to say something to my dad this morning, but he was so excited about the barn tour and then I got interested, too. My convertible wasn't a top priority."

Once again, Clay had been guilty of assumptions. He needed to stop making them when it came to Emily.

"We don't have time to fix it now, but if you'll get your keys, you can put it in the tractor barn so at least it's out of the sun. The tables and benches are stored down there, so drive on down and I'll meet you."

"Good idea." She glanced at the BMW. "It's eight years old, and things go wrong with it. My mom found it in the paper and thought I should have a classy car, but sometimes I think I'd be better off with something more practical."

Clay couldn't agree more, but he could tell the purchase had been more about pleasing her mother than pleasing herself. Emily Sterling didn't fit into the box he'd created for her, and that might put him on dangerous ground.

Ignoring her sexy body was one thing. Resisting a cry for help from someone who wasn't sure of her place in the world would be much more difficult. He'd been there, and no one should have to face that kind of insecurity alone.

4

EMILY FETCHED HER KEYS from her room and roasted her fanny driving the convertible down to the tractor barn. Maybe that was just as well. Searing her backside might serve as a reminder that little girls who moved too close to the fire could get burned.

No matter which way she looked at it, giving in to her instincts with Clay wouldn't be a good thing. Oh, except for the obvious, which involved glorious sex with a guy who had *hero* written all over him. The catch was just as obvious.

If her dad found out, no doubt he'd be disappointed in her. She couldn't imagine that he'd condone a superficial fling with Clay, and that's all it would amount to. She didn't want to disappoint her father any more than she already had.

Even worse, he might be disappointed with the apple of his eye, Clay Whitaker. The two men had a special relationship, and she had the power to ruin it. No doubt her dad had told Clay that a Wyoming man should steer clear of a California girl. Emmett certainly wouldn't want to see history repeating itself with his own daughter.

So she was faced with an afternoon in the company of a man she found wildly sexy, yet she couldn't do anything about it. To make matters even more complicated, he showed definite signs of a mutual attraction. She could tell by his heated looks, the tone of his voice and the occasional bulge in his jeans.

Knowing he didn't quite approve of her wasn't the turnoff for her that it should have been, either. No doubt about it, Clay would have preferred a cowgirl who fulfilled all of Emmett's unspoken dreams. Instead she was a city girl who spent her free time riding a surfboard instead of a horse.

Despite that, Clay wanted her, and Emily had the uncharitable urge to show him how a California surfer girl could destroy his control. Let him disapprove of her all he wanted—she'd bet that, given the opportunity, she could make him crazy with lust. It would be satisfying, indeed, if she could reduce him to begging for the chance to sink into her hot body.

She approached the large metal tractor barn. Clay had driven a dark blue pickup to the entrance and was letting down the tailgate as she drove past him. It was a simple task, so how come he looked so sexy doing it? She'd never made out in the bed of a pickup, but she wouldn't mind giving it a try with Clay.

By the time she pulled into the shadowed interior of the tractor barn, her hormones were dancing to a hip-hop beat and her noble intentions had taken a hike up the trail into the Grand Tetons. To hell with an uncomfortable truck bed. Her BMW was a four-passenger with a back-seat, and she was ready to invite Clay to join her there. But that was *such* a bad idea.

Gripping the leather-wrapped steering wheel, she closed her eyes and willed herself back to sanity. She'd driven here to celebrate her dad's sixtieth birthday, a major milestone. She would not muck it up by having sex with his protégé, no matter how yummy the guy was.

"Are you okay?"

She opened her eyes to find Mr. Yummy himself standing next to the driver's side of the car, his hat pushed back and his dark eyes filed with concern. For a split second she pictured telling him exactly what was on her mind, which involved getting naked and then squirming around on the warm leather upholstery of her car.

The tractor barn seemed empty of people other than the two of them, and if she'd judged their chemistry correctly, the event would be over in minutes with very little chance they'd be discovered *in flagrante delicto*. Of course, she wasn't figuring in birth control as part of this fantasy, and she didn't think Clay was the sort to be packing.

With a deep sigh, she gave up the whole concept. "I'm fine. The transition from the heat to the shade made me a little dizzy, is all."

He opened the car door for her and stood back. "You don't have to help me load the tables and benches. In fact, you don't have to help do any of this. I'll be back in a couple of hours and we can go riding then, if you still feel up to it."

"I want to help." She climbed out of the car and moved a safe distance away from him. As she'd suspected, they were very much alone in the cool and cavernous tractor barn.

"After all, this party is for my dad." She decided not to look directly at him and risk more eye contact. She was already on edge, and sexual tension wound tighter with every second they stood together inside the deserted barn. "Let's get started."

"Okay." His voice was suspiciously gruff. "You'll need these."

She had to look at him to find out what he meant by *these*. He was frowning as he held out a pair of leather work gloves.

That's when it occurred to her that he might not want to take her with him. She'd invited herself along, and with Sarah and Emmett jumping in to second the idea, he hadn't had much choice.

She didn't take the gloves. "Maybe I shouldn't go with you, after all. I don't know the routine and I might get in your way."

"But you said you wanted to."

"I know, but this isn't all about me. If my going will complicate things, then—"

"Take the gloves." His tone gentled. "I could use the help."

She hesitated a moment longer, and then decided that she really did want to be a part of setting up the party for her father. "All right. Thanks." She took the gloves and pulled them on. They were huge on her. Laughing, she held up both hands. "Look, Minnie Mouse."

He smiled. "Sorry. That's all I could find."

Instantly she was contrite. "I'm not complaining. I think it's sweet that you thought to give me gloves in the first place. They'll work fine." That's when she made the mistake of looking into his eyes, and the air went out of her lungs.

Oh…dear…God. She hadn't seen heat like that in… maybe she'd never seen heat like that. It was a wonder she didn't go up in flames. Parts of her felt as if they might combust at any moment.

Muttering a swear word under his breath, he dropped his gaze. "This is no good," he said, his voice husky.

"You're right. I won't go." She took off the gloves and held them out.

He lifted his head and looked at her. "That's not right, either."

"Sure it is." She shook the gloves. "Take these back, and I'll just go on up to the house."

He stared at the gloves. Then, with another muttered oath, he took them and tossed them into the front seat of her car.

"What on earth are you doing?"

"Making a mistake." He grasped both her wrists and drew her toward him.

She should have resisted. She didn't. Her heart beating furiously, she gulped as the distance between them grew smaller. "You don't want to do this."

"Oh, yes, I do." Releasing his hold on her wrist,

he took off his hat. That went into the front seat, too, followed by her hat.

"But you said it's no good." She began to tremble.

"It isn't." Sliding his hand around her waist, he pulled her into his arms. "Tell me to stop and I'll stop."

She couldn't believe any woman on the planet had that kind of willpower, especially when said woman had fantasized about the body she was now plastered against. Gazing into dark eyes that promised a thousand delights, she wanted every single one. She spread her hands over his muscled chest and felt his quick intake of breath and the staccato beat of his heart.

"One kiss." She struggled to breathe normally. "Surely we can handle that without causing a major problem."

"Right." His head dipped lower. "Maybe we won't like it."

Fat chance. "Maybe not." Her eyes fluttered closed.

"At least we should find out." His warm breath caressed her lips.

"We should." Anticipation shot fire through her veins. "But what if we like it?"

"We'll worry about that later." His lips settled over hers.

Nice, she thought. *We fit.* He tasted of cherry pie and coffee. She sighed with pleasure, wrapped her arms around his neck and leaned into him. This would be a good kiss. This would be—whoa! He changed the angle and delved deeper. The kiss intensified until the word *nice* no longer applied. *Wicked,* maybe or *wild,* or…

No words. She had no words for what he was doing

to her now. She opened wider, craving him as she'd never craved a man, demanding he give her more, and yet more…her nipples tightened and moisture gathered between her thighs. Digging her fingers into his shoulders, she arched against the bulge straining the fly of his jeans, and whimpered.

And then he stopped kissing her. Gasping, he held her tight and leaned his forehead against hers. "I was afraid of that."

"Kiss me again." She heard the plea in her voice and yet she couldn't help it. Sometime during the kiss she'd lost a sense of separateness, and now she could no longer tell whether the vibration she felt was her heart beating or his. She wanted to be caught up in the whirlwind once more, just once more.

He drew in a ragged breath. "If I kiss you again, we're going to end up naked on the nearest flat surface."

Her body hummed with excitement at the thought.

"And we both know that can't happen."

Slowly but inevitably, his words doused the fire raging inside her. Of course he was right. Loosening her grip on his broad shoulders, she eased out of his arms and took a couple of steps back.

She combed her fingers through her hair and flipped it over her shoulder as she gazed at him. "What now?"

Hands on his lean hips, he sent her an unhappy glance. "This is such a loaded situation that I don't even know where to start. Your dad trusts me. If I ended up seducing you, then—"

"Hold it right there, cowboy. I'm a big girl. That means no man is going to seduce me unless I want him to. The whole seduction issue cuts both ways. Let's say that *I* seduced *you*. That would be betraying my dad's trust, too, you know."

"I don't know how you figure that."

"Think about it. A beach-loving California girl gets involved with a dyed-in-the-wool Wyoming ranch hand. We know how that story turns out and so does my dad. He'd accuse me of being careless with the feelings of someone he loves like a son, someone who—" She stopped herself before she said "someone who was raised in a series of foster homes and probably has abandonment issues." He wouldn't appreciate her pop psychology evaluation.

Clay's smile was grim. "I'm a big boy. No woman seduces me unless I want her to."

She could almost see the shields going up around his heart. "That may be true, but my dad is not going to be happy no matter who is the seducer and who is the seducee. Both you and I know the story of his failed relationship, and he certainly expects us to be smarter than that."

"I thought I was, but…" He made a sweeping gesture with his hand. "You sorely tempt me, Emily Sterling."

"Ditto, Clay Whitaker." But if she hadn't fully considered it before, she now realized that a casual fling was the last thing a man like Clay needed. He'd had enough temporary relationships over the years. She didn't need to add her name to the list.

"Emmett wouldn't be happy to know about this attraction," Clay said.

"No, he would not." Emily met his gaze. "I guess we

have to make sure he doesn't find out, which means no more...no more..."

"Just no more," Clay said quietly. "No more, Emily. Like you said, we know the story wouldn't turn out well."

No, it wouldn't, but she wanted to lighten the mood. "That kiss was a humdinger, though."

"It was." He seemed to realize she wanted to end this on a teasing note. "I was hoping you were a slobbery kisser or that you would suck too hard on my tongue."

"You kissed me hoping I'd be bad at it? That's twisted."

He shrugged. "It would have solved my problem if you'd been a lousy kisser."

"I see." She gave him a long look. "For the record, I suck on tongues exactly the same way I suck on...other things."

He let out a low groan. "Now *that* was a low blow."

"You're the one who calculatingly kissed me hoping I would slobber on you or dislocate your tongue."

"I had to do something! You were driving me crazy with that traffic-stopping figure of yours and your cute little Minnie Mouse impersonation. A guy can take only so much, you know."

Satisfied she'd established an appropriately light and breezy mood, she let it drop. "All right. Let's call a truce and get those tables and benches loaded."

"You still want to come out there with me?"

"Yes, I do. Now that we've had this experience, and we've talked everything out, we both understand how we need to behave toward each other."

He raised his eyebrows. "Oh? And how is that, exactly?"

"Friendly, but not too friendly, if you know what I mean."

"I might."

"Accomplishing this job together will prove that we can interact without any hanky-panky."

"Fine. But you're not allowed to talk about how good you are at sucking…things."

"I promise not to discuss my sucking expertise."

"Good. The tables and benches are right over here." He started off, his long strides putting distance between them as he headed for a corner of the barn.

She picked up their hats and her gloves from the front seat of her car and followed him. She hoped they'd averted a disaster. He'd swept her away with that kiss, and if he hadn't called a halt, no telling what would have happened.

Yes, he'd made the first move, but he was a guy. Guys were conditioned to make the first move. She hadn't stopped him, and she could have. She should have. Clay had the body of a Greek god, but he could also have a heart of glass. She'd do well to remember that.

EMILY TURNED OUT TO BE a good and efficient worker. She did her share of the loading and made a couple of good suggestions for how to fit everything in. Once again, she'd surprised him by pitching in so eagerly. If he didn't know about the monthly checks she took from Emmett, he'd think she was a great person, someone he'd like having for a friend.

Maybe he'd have an opportunity to ask about those checks because that was the piece of the puzzle he didn't understand. He couldn't blame her for preferring the beach to the ranch. She'd been raised to think that way. But taking money from her father when he obviously wasn't a wealthy man—that made no sense at all.

Thinking about her accepting financial aid helped a little bit as he tried to ignore the enticing little droplets of sweat that rolled down her throat and into her cleavage. He reminded himself about those checks when she leaned over the tailgate and stretched the denim covering her delicious backside. She didn't have to do anything special to turn him on. Just looking at her got him hot.

He shouldn't have kissed her. Then again, the kiss might have worked to his advantage if he hadn't enjoyed it. Just because a woman was beautiful didn't mean she could kiss worth a damn. At least that's how he'd justified what had probably been a stupid move on his part.

Now he knew that she could kiss. She'd also informed him she could do other things with her mouth, things that he didn't need to be thinking about. Of course he couldn't seem to think about anything else, especially when she stopped to drink water from the canteen he handed her and fit her mouth around the opening. Damn.

He'd focused on the task at hand as best he could, and at last the truck was loaded. While Emily filled up the canteens, he tucked a couple of shovels in the back. He didn't know if she'd want to help dig the fire pits, but he'd offer her the chance. She seemed to enjoy physical labor.

Too bad for Emmett's sake that she didn't like ranching, because she had the kind of attitude that made for a good hand. She cheerfully accepted hard work and adapted to whatever conditions she found herself in. She didn't seem to mind getting dirty, either, which totally surprised him.

As she walked back to the truck with both canteens slung over her shoulder, he moved around to the passenger side and opened the door for her.

She turned that wonderful smile on him. "That's just so nice, Clay," she said as she climbed in. "I didn't realize how much I like having a man hold my chair and open my door for me."

"Like I said, Sarah deserves the credit. She won't tolerate sloppy manners from the men on her ranch." He felt guilty being praised for gentlemanly behavior when he'd taken full advantage of his position by the door to enjoy the snug fit of her jeans as she climbed in.

Under the circumstances he should be treating her like a kid sister and avoiding any sexual thoughts whatsoever. Yeah, right. She'd turned him on the first time he'd met her, and nothing had changed. If anything, his attention had become more intense.

God, he should never have kissed her. What had he been thinking? He hadn't been thinking—that was the answer. He'd walked over to her car and seen her sitting in it with her eyes closed and her hands clenched around the steering wheel.

Instantly he'd worried that she was sick, and with

Emmett gone, he was responsible for her well-being. But then she'd opened her eyes and he'd known right away that she wasn't sick. No, she was sexually aroused. And it didn't take a genius to know he was the lucky guy who'd created that situation.

They'd managed to feed each other's fires until he couldn't stand it another second. He shouldn't have reacted that way, and he should probably regret that he'd shoved aside his misgivings and kissed her. But he didn't regret it. That kiss was the way kisses should always be—a trip to the sun and back.

He made sure she was tucked inside before he closed the door of the truck. Then he walked around to the driver's side. He'd left the keys in the ignition, a common habit around the ranch. Sliding in behind the wheel, he began to understand the mess he was in.

Just sitting next to her in the cab was going to be torture. The air-conditioning didn't work in this truck, and the heat from her body amplified the impact of her perfume. A whiff of sea and sand mingled with the scent of a healthy, sexy woman to create an aromatic cocktail that could get him drunk in no time.

Maybe with the windows down, he'd manage to survive the trip without pulling over and reaching for her. He started the truck.

"How far away is the spot where we'll have the cookout?"

"Not far." But with her sitting right next to him, it might turn out to be the longest damn drive of his life.

5

"I DON'T THINK I'VE EVER been on this road." Emily focused on the scenery, which somewhat distracted her from the virile cowboy in the driver's seat, the one she longed to kiss again, but would not.

So instead she admired the wildflowers that created a carpet of purple, yellow and white in the meadows they passed. She watched flocks of birds fly away at their approach and rabbits hop into the underbrush by the side of the road. She'd been on trail rides with her dad, but she'd been so determined not to like Wyoming that she'd missed its beauty.

Ahead of them, the snow that still remained on the summit of the Grand Tetons glittered in the sun. She'd never been here in the winter and had never tried skiing, although she had friends who loved it. She'd avoided finding anything positive about Jackson Hole, and that was a shame.

"Emmett never took you out to the sacred site?" Clay had to talk over the noise of the engine and the tables and benches rattling in the back.

"No, I would have remembered that." She felt sad that her father hadn't mentioned the landmark, but she didn't blame him. She hadn't been particularly enthusiastic about any of the local attractions, so why should he? Maybe she was finally old enough to realize that she didn't have to keep harping on her love of all things California. By now, Emmett got it.

"This road leads to the site." Clay avoided a particularly deep rut. "We'll have the cookout in the meadow east of there."

"What's sacred about the place?"

"There's a big flat rock about the size of a parking space there. The stone is gray granite with white streaks of quartz through it."

"Sounds pretty."

"It is, especially when the sun or the moon shines on it. Then the quartz sparkles."

Emily laughed. "That works for me. I like shiny, sparkly things."

"We'll stop on the way back so you can take a look. Back when Archie and Nelsie were alive, the Shoshone Indians used to worship on that spot, so they've always been allowed on the property. But I don't think the Shoshone have been there for years."

"It's for religious services?"

"Well, not exactly."

"What, then?"

He glanced over at her. "According to the Shoshone legend, if you have an issue to resolve or uncertainties in your life, being on that rock will give you clarity. Morgan's parents—have you met Morgan?"

"Not yet. Tomorrow night I'm supposed to meet everyone."

"Anyway, her parents are into all the New Age stuff, so Morgan knows about it, too. She says that quartz is supposed to be a powerful crystal."

"I've heard that. One of my surfer friends is into crystals." Emily could think of at least two issues she wouldn't mind having clarity on. Her purpose in life would be one. The other one was sitting next to her. "Have you ever tried it?"

He didn't answer right away, which told her that he probably had tried it and didn't want to admit that he had.

"It's okay," she said. "I'm from California, remember? The land of woo-woo. I just want to know if this rock works or not. I could use some clarity in my life."

"I came out here a few months after I'd landed the job working for the Chances. I wanted to know if it would last."

"The job?"

"I suppose, but I wanted to know more than that. A job was one thing. But I was starting to become attached to the people—Sarah, Jonathan, Emmett. I wanted to know if I'd finally…"

She sensed this had been an important moment for him and he didn't share it with many people. She felt honored he'd even considered sharing it with her. "Finally what?" she prompted gently.

He blew out a breath. "If I'd finally found a home."

Her heart ached for him. Of course he'd longed for some permanent place that would always welcome him. That was the thing he'd been denied his whole life. "Did…did the sacred site give you an answer?"

"Sort of. Something that had been knotted up in me seemed to relax, and I took that to be a good sign. Then a raven flew over and pooped on my shirt." He laughed. "I'm not sure what that was supposed to mean."

"That's easy. Shit happens."

"Maybe that was the message. Anyway, the Chance family, along with Emmett, have given me a home base, so whether the rock was telling me that or not, my life has worked out so far."

"I'm glad. You know, if my dad had been willing to move to Santa Barbara like my mother wanted him to, he wouldn't have been here when you came to the ranch."

He looked over at her. "You mean like that saying, that things happen for a reason?"

"Sort of, yeah."

"That hardly seems fair." He frowned. "I don't like the idea that you had to give him up so that I could have him."

She was tempted to say that Clay might have needed her dad more than she had, but she decided against it. No man liked to appear weaker than a woman, even psychologically. "In any case, if he couldn't be with me, then I'm glad he was here for you."

Clay drove along silently for several minutes. Finally he spoke again. "Do you believe that saying?"

"Which one?"

"That things happen for a reason."

She thought about it. "I guess I do. For the most part, anyway. Why?"

"Then please tell me why you and I have run into each other again this summer. If there's a reason besides torturing me with things I can't have, I'd love to know what it is."

He spoke with such feeling that she was taken aback. "Am I really torturing you?"

"Not on purpose, I'm sure. Wait, I take that back. Your comment about your sucking ability was absolutely on purpose, and I've been tortured by that ever since."

"I shouldn't have said that."

"So *now* you realize it, when it's too late to do anything about it."

She leaned back against the headrest and controlled the urge to smile as a very naughty idea came to her. "Maybe it's not really too late."

"Oh, yes, it is." His tone was heated and tinged with desperation. "In case you've forgotten, we've already had this discussion. From now on we're going to be friendly, but not *too* friendly. In other words, it's too late."

She couldn't stop herself from grinning. This could be a real adventure, something she'd never offered a man in quite this way before. And it wouldn't count as an actual fling. "Come on now, Clay. What's a little oral sex between friends?"

He swerved to the side of the road and hit the brakes so hard the load in back rumbled in protest. *"What?"*

She turned her head to look at him. "Think of it as

a friendly gesture to keep you from going off the deep end. You just admitted that I'm torturing you."

"Yeah, but—"

"Since it's my fault for putting that thought in your mind and now you're struggling with sexual frustration, then it seems only fair that I relieve your condition so that you can continue on about your business."

He stared at her, his eagerness evident in the strained fabric of his jeans, but his gaze wary. "What…what about our plan not to get involved with each other?"

"I'm not proposing marriage, or even an affair." The more she thought about this, the more she liked the idea. "I'm simply offering an answer to your problem. Nobody ever has to know."

"I can't believe you're saying this."

"Can you believe I would do it?"

His breathing quickened. "Yes, I sure as hell can, and that's what's driving me insane. I've had an X-rated movie going in my head ever since you broached the subject in the barn."

Taking off her hat, she set it on the dash. Then she unbuckled her seat belt and turned toward him. "I should never have teased you with that remark. Let me make it up to you."

"I'm not sure this is a good idea."

She glanced at his crotch. "You're being outvoted."

"No surprise there." His chest heaved as he dragged in a breath.

"It's a reasonable solution." She rested her hand on his thigh and felt the muscles bunch. Excitement churned through her at the thought of what she wanted to do. "And it won't take long."

He closed his eyes and leaned his head back. "That's a given."

Slowly, as if approaching a wild animal, she reached for his zipper. "You need this, Clay."

"Yes," he murmured. As the zipper rasped in the stillness, he groaned. *"Yes."*

HE COULDN'T BELIEVE HE WAS allowing her to do this, but the way she'd explained it made some crazy kind of sense. She *was* responsible for his inflamed state, and she'd suggested helping him out by performing exactly what she'd hinted was her specialty. If he didn't take that pleasure now, he'd never have another chance.

She was right that no one ever had to know. He'd suffer through slivers under his fingernails before he'd tell anybody about *this*. He squeezed his eyes shut and groaned as she fumbled her way through the unveiling, and then…oh, man.

This was frickin' *incredible*. Her warm fingers wrapped around what felt like the most intense hard-on he'd ever had in his life. She'd volunteered to ease his pain, and only an idiot would pass up the opportunity.

Grateful didn't even begin to describe his state of mind. But when her breath whispered across the head of his cock, he had no state of mind. He had no mind, period.

He braced himself for contact, tightening his hands into fists and clenching his jaw. He'd always prided himself on his control, and he'd need every bit of it when she...ahhh...heaven. Her tongue. Licking. Stroking. Teasing. So good, so very, very...*good*. She deserved those bragging rights.

Someone moaned. Could've been him. He wanted to open his eyes. Didn't dare. And yet, he wanted to see, wanted the visual. To keep forever.

Had to risk it. Had to look. Holding his breath, he watched the golden top of her head as she lowered her mouth down over his cock. Her hair curtained her face, tickling him as she lifted up again, curling into her mouth, getting in her way.

She pushed the damp strands away. Then she tried to pull her hair back with her free hand, but it wouldn't stay. She made an impatient sound low in her throat.

The vibration from that sound nearly made him come, but he conquered the urge, because he knew what needed to be done. Unclenching both fists, he scooped her silky hair back and held it at the nape of her neck.

And now...now he could watch. Her cheeks hollowed and her eyelashes fluttered as she moved rhythmically up and down, up and down, up...his control slipped a notch...and down...up...she did something with her tongue and he gasped...down...once more...and up... blood rushed in his ears...*now*.

With a ragged cry, he came, his cock pulsing inside her warm mouth. She sucked more vigorously as she swallowed, and swallowed again. Pleasure rolled over him in waves so strong he was afraid he might pass out.

But he didn't, and gradually the world came into focus and he slumped against the seat. A raven perched on the hood of the truck and stared at him. Good thing a bird hadn't flown in the open windows of the cab, although he might not have noticed. A bear could have tried to climb in and he might not have noticed.

Emily released him gently with lingering kisses, and then she tucked his johnson carefully back into his jeans. He realized he was still gripping her hair, caveman style. He let go and she sat up.

"Emily, that—" He sounded like a rusty hinge, so he cleared his throat and tried again. "That was unbelievable."

She smiled and combed her hair back from her face. Her green eyes sparkled and her lipstick was gone, but her mouth was rosy from all that activity. "Better, now?"

"You have no idea."

"See how easy that was? Problem solved, and nobody has to be the wiser."

"You can damned well count on me not to say anything." Now that he was recovering from his state of bliss, he noticed that although his breathing had returned to normal, hers hadn't. The rapid rise and fall of her breasts brought his attention to another fact—under her T-shirt and bra, her nipples were standing at attention.

"My lips are sealed," she said. "It's our little secret."

Intrigued with his new thought, he studied her. Her cheeks were flushed and when his glance traveled over her, she shivered slightly. "Emily, I'm thinking that by solving my problem, you've created one for yourself."

"What do you mean?"

"Maybe now you're the one jacked up on sexual frustration."

She waved a hand dismissively. "Maybe just a little. No problemo."

"That's not fair. Do you want me to—"

"No!" She drew back against the door. "I mean, no, thank you, although it's kind of you to offer."

"It's not kindness that prompted me. I want to." Now that he understood what had happened, his fingers itched to slide inside her panties and return the favor.

"It's a bad idea. One little episode like we just had can be pushed under the rug. Making out all afternoon—not so much. We could slide right into a full-blown affair if we're not careful, and the more we get involved, the more likely we'll be found out. Besides, we have work to do."

"That's a fact. But if we skip the horseback ride, then we'd have time for me to even the score." And he'd love to do that. Giving her a climax now seemed like a most excellent concept, and no one would ever have to know about that, either.

She shook her head. "We're already even. I created a problem for you and now I've taken care of it. We need to move on."

"What's the matter? Are you afraid to let me see you lose control the way I just did?"

"Of course not! I'm trying to minimize our involvement. Anyway, giving a guy an orgasm just involves unzipping his pants. With a woman it's more complicated."

"Not really." He was growing impatient with her stubborn refusal.

"It is, too, more complicated. Your…equipment is all external. Mine's internal."

"Insignificant details."

"Anatomically speaking, it's not insignificant at all."

"Practically speaking, it is. I might have to unfasten your belt and unbutton your jeans, but that takes no time. I'm a cowboy. I know my way around a pair of women's britches."

"I'm sure you do."

"All I need is room to maneuver." He gave her a lazy smile. "If you'd said yes five minutes ago instead of arguing with me, you'd be having an orgasm right now." He watched the pupils in her eyes dilate as desire gripped her. "What do you say?"

"No." She swallowed. "Please start the truck."

"I think you'd really like it."

"That's not the point. We need to draw the line somewhere. What's done is done, and we can put it behind us and forget about it."

He stared at her in disbelief. "You expect me to forget about it?"

"Why not? It was one quick climax to lower your stress level, not much different from a sneeze or a cough. No big deal."

"*A sneeze or a cough?* You're kidding, right?"

"Studies have shown that a good sneeze is very similar to—"

"You're seriously telling me that you'd just as soon sneeze as come?"

She looked away, her color high. "Well, that may be a slight exaggeration. My only point is that a climax isn't that big a deal."

"If you say so." He straightened and reached for the ignition. "But then, I'm willing to bet you've never had one courtesy of a cowboy."

6

EMILY HAD PLENTY OF TIME to think about cowboys and climaxes during the next two hours. After she and Clay unloaded the tables and benches, they collected piles of rocks to line the fire pits. Then she threw herself into the job of digging the smaller one in hopes the sweaty labor would eliminate her desire for sex with the gorgeous guy working a few yards away.

No dice. While shoveling, she tried to distract herself by concentrating on her natural environment. But the scent of warm grass and the distant gurgle of a creek only reminded her that she was alone in this glorious place with a man who'd offered to give her pleasure. Even though she wouldn't allow herself to look directly at him, she was aware of every move he made.

Finally, when the pit seemed deep enough, she laid down her shovel and rewarded herself with a quick glance in Clay's direction. Oh, dear God. He'd taken off his shirt.

Considering his parting shot, he'd probably done it on purpose. She couldn't be sure of that, because it was hot work. If she could have taken off her shirt she would have. Women weren't given the same leeway to strip down, though, and that left her overheated both inside and out.

A smart woman would save herself some grief by turning away from the rhythmic flex of biceps, pecs and delts every time Clay drove his shovel into the ground. Emily wasn't very smart since she couldn't stop staring. Obviously he'd worked shirtless at other times over the summer, because his skin had been kissed to a golden hue by the Wyoming sun.

Tossing his shovel aside, he began lining the pit with rocks, which meant he had to lean down. A lot. Each time, the soft denim of his jeans pulled tight across his picture-perfect ass.

Emily tingled all over. *Oh, baby.*

As if sensing her ogling, he looked at her, his face shadowed by his hat brim, his expression unreadable. "Tired?"

Tired of being noble. "A little bit, I guess."

"Then take a break. You've done plenty, and I can finish up with the rocks. Go on over to the truck and relax."

"Maybe I will." But if she stopped working she'd have nothing to do but watch him, and that wouldn't help her condition at all. She pointed to a faint set of tire tracks leading toward the line of trees. "Does this go to the creek?"

"Yep. If you can hang on for a few more minutes, I'll drive us over there and you can splash some cool water on your face."

Her face wasn't the main area that needed cool water, but she wasn't about to tell him. "If you don't mind, I'll walk on over now."

He shrugged. "Suit yourself. Just follow the tracks and they'll take you straight to the bank of the creek. I'll pick you up when I'm done. And thanks for all your help, Emily. You're a hard worker."

"You sound surprised."

"To be honest, I am a little bit surprised."

That irritated her. He might be yummilicious with his bronzed shoulders gleaming in the sun, but she couldn't let him get away with insulting her. "Look, I may not have a college degree and a career plan, but that doesn't mean I don't know how to work."

"It's not about school or jobs. It's…" He paused, braced his hands on his hips and blew out a breath.

"Spit it out, cowboy. You've come this far, so you might as well get it off your chest." *Your incredibly muscled chest.*

"Hell, this is none of my damned business, but I like you, and I can't figure out why, when you're perfectly capable of supporting yourself, you still take money from your dad every month."

She stared at him. "What in hell are you talking about?"

"I'm talking about the checks he sends you. That money might seem like nothing to you, but it's a good portion of his paycheck."

She folded her arms, so ready to take this cowboy down several notches. "You have no idea what you're talking about. That money doesn't come out of his paycheck. It's part of my inheritance from my grandparents."

He hesitated for a moment, but then he shook his head. "That can't be right. The ranch is a small place. Somebody would know about an inheritance."

"He's a private man. Which brings up my first question. How do you know he sends me money? Are you two so close that he confides all his financial secrets?" She didn't like the idea that Clay was privy to things even she didn't know.

"It's not just me. We all know. Even though he gets a decent salary, he never has spare cash, and it didn't take a genius to figure out he was still mailing checks to California."

She went from angry to horrified. "Are you saying that everyone at the Last Chance thinks I'm sponging off my father?"

"Well, yeah, but—"

"That's *awful!* I'm surprised anyone's nice to me."

His voice gentled. "They're nice to you because of Emmett."

She closed her eyes in dismay. Then slowly she opened them again. "And I suppose no one has thought to tell my dad that they think his daughter is a spoiled brat who's soaking him."

"Of course not. Why would we? That's why I asked you about it. You don't seem like the kind of person who would do that."

"I'm not that kind of person! It's an inheritance!"

"How do you know that?"

"Because he told me. Are you now claiming my father's a liar?"

"No, I'm not. But it doesn't add up, Emily. The guy never has extra money, and it seems like his parents would have left him something, too, especially if they trusted him enough to manage your inheritance."

She wished his logic didn't make so much sense. "He's not the type to spend on himself, that's all. Maybe he's tucked his portion away in a bank."

"I don't think so."

"And I don't think you're qualified to have that opinion, unless you've been peeking at his bank statements."

Clay sighed. "I haven't, and neither has anyone else. But we all know that he refuses to marry Pam Mulholland because she has more money than he does, so if he has some inheritance stashed away, then—"

"They're that serious?" Emily's stomach tightened. Sure, her parents had the right to find somebody else, especially after all these years, but again, that was logic talking.

"I think they might be in love, if that's what you mean. But your dad's old-fashioned, and doesn't like the idea of marrying somebody who's better off financially."

"This is crazy. None of it makes sense."

He stepped closer. "I can see you're upset, and I'm sorry. But I couldn't keep quiet after the way you've been working this afternoon. Your actions don't fit the reputation you have around here."

"Thank you." The concern in his dark eyes comforted her, but the nearness of his sweaty, virile body threatened to obliterate her good sense. She had a sudden vivid image of sex on a picnic table. That was a bad idea on so many levels, with the most obvious one being a lack of birth control.

He gave her a wry smile. "You know, in some ways it would have been easier on me if you'd been a brat."

"Sorry to disappoint you." She'd better get out of here before the chemistry between them took complete control of the situation. "Listen, I'm going to walk to the creek and think about this. I obviously need to have a discussion with my dad, but—"

"Tomorrow's his birthday."

"Right. I mean, maybe there really is an inheritance, but I tend to think you're right that he made it up, for whatever reason. Confronting him with this won't be easy for either him or me."

"No, probably not." His voice was rich with compassion.

Hearing that compassion was a turn-on. Or maybe hearing him recite the alphabet would be a turn-on. Still, he was the only sounding board she had right now, and listening to his reaction might help her figure out what to do.

"There's something else," she said. "I've banked all the money instead of spending it."

"All of it?"

"Yes." She peered up at him. "Is that so hard to believe?"

"It shouldn't be, now that I know you better, but I would have expected you to spend at least part of it."

"So will he, and he may be upset that I haven't. But

at eighteen I had no clue what I wanted to do with my life. At twenty-seven, I still don't know. I wanted to save the money until I had a better chance of spending it wisely, whether it's for a college degree or to start my own business."

"You must have a fair amount tucked away by now."

This part of her life she could be proud of. "I seem to have a knack for investing, so I've done well with what he's sent me over the years." She paused. "But I'm not sure how he'll take any of this, so can we…can we keep this conversation just between us for now?"

He nodded. "That's a given. But don't you want to set the record straight with everyone at the ranch?"

"I'd love to, but my dad comes ahead of worrying about what everyone else thinks of me, so I want to proceed with care."

"Understood."

"All right, then." She resisted the urge to touch him. Even a small gesture like putting her hand on his arm could ignite the passion smoldering just beneath the surface of their seemingly calm discussion. "Are you sure you don't need me to stay and help finish up with the rocks?"

"I'm sure. Take some time alone to think this through."

"Okay. See you soon." She turned and began walking down the widest of the two tire tracks through the meadow.

"I'll drive over shortly," he called after her.

"Thanks!" She hoped that by the time he did, she'd

have some plan for dealing with her father. But she also needed a plan to deal with Clay.

Now she realized why he'd had that prickly edge to him. He hadn't liked being attracted to someone he didn't approve of. Now that he knew she wasn't taking advantage of Emmett, he had no reason to dislike her. As he'd said, she'd made it tougher for him.

Tougher for herself, too. Still, they might make it through without giving in to their feelings for each other. As he'd said before, he didn't want to risk damaging his relationship with Emmett. Besides, she was no psychologist, but she had to believe that, as a former foster kid, Clay would want to avoid anyone who was guaranteed to leave him.

Those two issues loomed larger the more distance she put between her and the dark-eyed cowboy. Their problems arose when they spent too much time near each other, and the concerns that should keep them apart… didn't. She couldn't do much to prevent their close proximity for the next hour or so, but once they'd returned to the ranch, she'd keep out of the danger zone.

She reached the trees about the time she had that thought, and stepped gratefully into the shade. She caught the flash of a sunlit patch of water through the maze of trunks and headed for the liquid sound the creek made as it slid over rocks and fallen branches. Somewhere she'd read that cascading water gave people a more positive outlook.

Maybe the creek would help her mood as she considered how to broach the money subject with her dad. She'd wait until the day after his birthday, though. He'd probably be embarrassed that he'd been caught in a lie he'd been telling her for nine years.

She wasn't sure what had motivated him to disguise the checks as an inheritance, but she could guess. He wanted to guarantee that she'd take the money without guilt. Her dad knew all about guilt. Apparently he'd blamed himself for being an absentee father, and sending her money every month soothed his conscience.

But when he found out that she'd touched none of it, how would that affect him? She didn't know for sure, but she was afraid he'd take it as a rejection of his loving gesture. And all the guilt he'd sloughed off as a result of sending those checks would come roaring back.

No, she couldn't bring up the subject until after his birthday. Sarah had gone to a great deal of trouble to make the celebration special, and Emily would be a most ungrateful houseguest to ride in and spoil it all. That would show her to be easily as selfish as everyone thought she was.

She reached the creek and sat down on a fallen log to take off her boots. Until today she hadn't worn them for more than five minutes, and they weren't broken in. Dangling her feet in the water seemed like an excellent idea.

Leaving her boots and her borrowed hat by the log, she looked for a place on the bank that would allow her to sit, but no log or branch had fallen into a convenient position and the rocks were wet. If she wanted to put her feet in the water, she'd have to wade in. So be it. She rolled up her jeans and edged down the embankment.

She gasped as her toes made contact with the icy

creek, but as a surfer, she could take the cold. She also had excellent balance, so standing on smooth stones while the water rippled around her was child's play.

As she congratulated herself on solving her problem of achy, sore feet, she glanced across the creek—which was only about as wide as an average hotel room—and came eyeball-to-eyeball with an SUV-sized bull moose. At least, she assumed it was a bull moose. He looked a little bit like Bullwinkle, and his antlers could have served as a coatrack for a family of six, which probably meant this was a male.

She stood very still, and so did the moose. He seemed as surprised to meet her as she was to meet him, but Emily thought the moose had the advantage in this encounter. She vaguely remembered news stories of people being trampled by a large moose, but hadn't that been in Alaska?

This was a Wyoming moose, and she could hope that they were friendlier. Maybe the only thing this guy wanted was a cold drink. So far as she was concerned, he could drain the creek dry. She would just stand there, not moving.

The moose, however, didn't seem willing to stay on his side of the stream. When he stepped into the water with what Emily now viewed as killer hooves, she panicked and tried to move backward on the slippery rocks. She went down in a very ungraceful sideways move that tossed her into deeper water.

That could be a good thing. A moose might not be able to trample her to death in three feet of water. Still, she could certainly drown in that depth if she didn't get her head out soon.

Flailing to the surface might not be wise with Bullwinkle around, but she had this little issue of breathing. Grabbing at mossy rocks, she managed to get her head up far enough to gulp for air and take a quick moose survey. No Bullwinkle.

Getting out of the creek while wearing soggy jeans and a T-shirt was tricky, but she managed it right as Clay appeared. Of course he'd show up while she was in the middle of making a fool of herself. He'd put his shirt on but hadn't fastened the snaps, so his glorious chest was still fully visible when he hurried forward and the breeze caught and parted the material.

"What happened?" He offered his hand to help her up the embankment.

"Would you believe I was pushed by a moose?"

"I thought I heard something crashing through the trees when I got out of the truck. You must have scared the hell out of him."

"Oh, yeah." Emily found solid footing and paused to shove her dripping hair out of her eyes. "I had him on the run, no question."

Clay released her hand and stepped back to survey the damage. "I have a blanket in the truck."

"That would be nice." A blanket sounded good right now, but it could lead to…several things. She decided not to think about the various options, for fear she'd become invested in one of those outcomes.

Now that she was out of the water, her clammy clothes felt icky and cold. If Clay hadn't been right there, she would have peeled them off, but she wasn't supposed to be doing anything that could be construed as sexual. Removing clothes could easily be interpreted as an invitation.

In truth, she wouldn't mind making such an invitation, if only her conscience would check out for a while. She was shivery and he looked warm and cozy. More than that, she could tell by the gleam in his eyes that he still wanted her, and that was reassuring, considering that she must look like a bedraggled mess.

He gazed at her a moment longer, and then glanced around. "Where are your boots and hat?"

"Over by that log." She pointed to the spot, but her wet jeans were so heavy she felt cemented to the ground.

As if he understood that completely, he walked over and grabbed her stuff. "Hold these."

She took everything, and before she realized what he had in mind, he'd swept her dripping self up in his arms and moved off through the trees as if he carried women all the time. She felt silly being thrilled by such a macho gesture, but her romantic, little heart loved it.

Still, she was a modern woman with modern sensibilities. "You don't have to do this," she said as he tromped through the underbrush, crushing leaves and twigs under his boots. "I can walk."

"No, you can't. Going barefoot in the forest is a really bad idea, and your jeans are so wet you'd probably stain the leather of those top-of-the-line Ropers. I can't stand to see a good pair of boots suffer."

She laughed. "So this has nothing to do with me and everything to do with my boots."

"Oh, I wouldn't say that."

"Meaning?"

"Meaning that once I get you to the truck, you'll want to take off those wet clothes and wrap up in the blanket. I have a strong suspicion that somewhere in that process, we're going to get very friendly."

Desire slammed into her with the force of a medicine ball in the gut. She glanced up at him, but all she could see was his very determined profile. "That's not a good idea."

"Probably not, but there's an air of inevitability about it. Besides, no one should go through life believing that an orgasm is no different than a sneeze. That's just pitiful."

7

CLAY HAD APPROACHED THE CREEK with the best of intentions. Emily was absolutely right that any sexual move on his part would raise the stakes. In the afterglow of the amazing climax she'd given him, he hadn't cared. But digging a fire pit and hauling rocks tended to steady a guy and help him face reality.

In his case, facing reality meant staying away from Emily Sterling. Now that he had his degree and a great job, he was ripe for commitment, but his dream girl would love ranching and specifically love the Last Chance. Sarah Chance had already told Clay that he could have a little plot of ranch land whenever the domestic urge hit.

He could see that day coming soon, although he hadn't dated anyone since moving back to Jackson Hole. He might want to remedy that so that he wouldn't be susceptible to a beautiful woman like Emily—the wrong woman who'd shown up at the right time.

His mind had been clear and focused until he'd arrived to discover that she'd fallen into the damn creek.

His mind was still clear, but it was focused on an entirely different goal. As he carried her back to where he'd parked the truck, he tried to imagine getting through the next thirty minutes without touching her naked body. Sadly, he wasn't that strong.

If only she didn't want him as much as he wanted her, then maybe he could have ignored this opportunity. But she did want him. He could tell by the way she wrapped her free arm around his shoulders and pressed her body close. Her heat penetrated her wet clothes so thoroughly that he wouldn't be surprised to see steam rising as he strode through the woods.

"I'm turning into a lot of trouble, huh?" She shifted her weight and snuggled against him.

He stifled a groan as his cock responded. "Yeah, you sure are."

"Would you believe I drove over here to spread sunshine and love?"

"Yep." The navy blue pickup came into view. "You spread quite a bit of it when you unzipped my jeans this afternoon."

"You're really not going to forget that, are you?"

"Never."

"Never? Oh, come on. Aren't you being a little too dramatic?"

He walked around to the back of the truck. "Emily, a guy might forget a woman's birthday or the loaf of bread he was supposed to bring home from the store, but he'll never forget a spectacular blow job."

"Oh."

"That's my Guide to Guys tip for the day." He paused

at the rear of the truck. "Now just sit tight on the bumper while I get the blanket." He eased her down to the chrome-plated surface. "Is it too hot?"

"No, actually, it feels good."

He imagined warmth working itself through her wet jeans to the part of her body he was personally focused on. The warm bumper might give her a jump start on pleasure. "I'll take your boots and hat."

She handed them over and glanced up at him, her green eyes mischievous. "So it was spectacular, huh?"

He met her gaze. "You've set the bar pretty high, but that's okay. I'm up to the challenge." As he walked around to the cab and deposited her hat and boots inside, he wondered if she'd been able to tell that he was just plain *up*, period. The prospect of caressing her until she came apart in his arms was causing his johnson some discomfort, but without condoms, he'd have to ignore that side effect.

"I've never agreed to a thing, you know," she called out from her perch. "I can ride home in the truck bed so I won't get the seat wet. No blanket required."

He took that for token resistance and grabbed the old wool blanket from behind the seat. "Emmett would never forgive me." He carried the blanket to the back of the truck. "But it's up to you. Is that what you want?"

She'd finger-combed her wet hair and she looked like the winning contestant in a wet T-shirt contest. For all the good her bra and shirt were doing her, she might as well be naked. That idea sounded good to him.

"I don't want to get you in trouble with my dad," she said. "Or get me in trouble, either, for that matter. Let's face it, I'm here for the short term. With your…background, that makes me a liability to…to your mental health."

Clay sighed. "So you're worried about me because I was a poor foster kid, is that it?"

"Well…yeah."

"Do me a favor and forget that, okay? I'm not an emotional cripple, and I can handle this situation just fine."

She gazed at him. "All right."

"So now we're back to you. What do *you* want?"

"What I want is to get out of these miserable clothes ASAP. But even if I take them off now, they won't magically get dry in time, so what have I gained?"

He smiled. "Something I can guarantee you'll never forget, either."

"You're incorrigible." Her reprimand didn't have much punch to it, especially considering the glow of excitement in her green eyes. "You and I both know I can't go back to the ranch wearing nothing but a blanket." She swung her bare feet back and forth.

He noticed purple toenail polish and realized he liked that she was playful when it came to such things. "Sure you can, especially if you have on underwear. And in this heat, your bra and panties will dry in no time."

"You mean while I'm wearing them?"

He didn't mean that and she damn well knew it, but he'd play the game. "They'll dry a hell of a lot faster draped over the tailgate." He held her gaze so that she wouldn't mistake his meaning. While her underwear dried, he'd be doing his level best to make her very, very wet.

"You're seriously suggesting I walk back into the house wrapped in a blanket?"

"Why not? You fell in the creek and then used the blanket to protect your modesty while you took off your shirt and jeans so you wouldn't get the upholstery all wet."

"And you think everyone will buy that?"

"In the first place, you might be lucky enough to make it upstairs without being seen. Even if you are seen, it won't matter as long as you treat it like an accident you had to handle in the best way you could. But I can guarantee that if I haul you home in the back of the pickup, I'll hear about it from your dad. That's not how a cowboy treats a lady."

She studied him for several seconds. At last she seemed to come to a decision. "How does a cowboy treat a lady?"

He let out a long, slow breath. "Let me show you."

"But what if somebody comes?"

He just grinned. No need to say a single thing.

"I didn't mean it like *that*. What if somebody shows up here while we're…involved?"

His heart hammered in anticipation. She was considering it. "Highly unlikely."

"Then…yes."

Glory, hallelujah, he'd won. He might regret this later, but at the moment he was filled with jubilation. She would go along with the plan, and his insides did a victory dance. He started forward, but she held up her hand like a traffic cop.

"I'll take care of the beginning stages." She reached for the hem of her T-shirt and, to his delight, peeled it off over her head. Because the shirt was so wet, he'd known in advance that her bra was a white lacy affair that offered a tantalizing glimpse of her nipples, tight as wild raspberries under the confining lace.

Even so, his heart hammered at the prospect of touching her there, of drawing a taut nipple into his mouth and rolling it with his tongue… He was so mesmerized by the prospect that he almost missed the T-shirt when she tossed it at him. But he'd played basketball at a community youth center when he was a kid, and his reflexes were still decent. He caught the wadded-up shirt in one hand.

"It feels so great to have that gone!" She stretched her arms over her head. "Now for the jeans. If I stand on the bumper, will you help me get them off?"

He laughed. "Oh, yeah." He realized that somehow she'd managed to turn the tables on him. He'd intended to seduce her, but it seemed to be going the other way. "But stand on the same spot where you've been sitting, so the chrome won't be so hot."

"Good idea." Swinging her legs up onto the bumper, she took hold of the tailgate and pulled herself to a standing position with her back to him. "I'm steadier turned this way. If I hold on, can you just—"

"You bet. Glad to help." Laying the folded blanket on the end of the bumper and his hat on top of that, he reached around and worked at the metal button, that didn't want to go through the wet buttonhole.

"If you'll hold on to me, I can try," she said.

"Nope. I've about got it. There it goes." He took hold of the zipper, which wasn't easy to deal with, either, but at last he was able to slide the jeans over her hips.

Only thing was, her panties wanted to come along for the ride. What the hell. She'd planned to take them off anyway.

As he exposed her smooth skin, she sucked in a breath.

"Can't help it," he muttered. "Everything's stuck together."

"Mmm."

His pulse quickened. She had such a curvy, tempting backside. Before he'd quite realized what he intended to do, he'd leaned over and pressed his mouth against her cool skin.

"Clay…"

He couldn't tell whether she'd said his name as a protest or a plea. But when he flicked his tongue over the same spot, she whimpered in a way that removed all doubt. Green light. He nibbled and kissed his way across the small of her back as he moved to her other silken cheek.

The scent of arousal called to him, and he slipped his hand between her thighs. She was still trapped in her jeans, so he didn't have much room to maneuver, but he couldn't resist. There. He found her moist entrance and her hot trigger point.

Her ragged breathing told him that he could make her

come in seconds. But that wasn't his plan. He didn't want her to climax while tangled in wet denim. So he teased her lightly, all the while placing kisses on her delicious bottom. Then he withdrew his hand and savored the impatient noise she made in the back of her throat.

"Not yet," he murmured as he peeled her jeans and panties down to her ankles. "Step out."

She did, and he shoved them aside. They fell on the ground, but he was past caring about that. "Turn around. I'll help you."

He steadied her by holding on to her waist as she pivoted on one bare foot and found purchase with the other. He would never forget the sight of her purple toenails as she braced her feet on the chrome bumper.

Slowly his gaze traveled upward, past her tanned, shapely legs to a spot that had never seen the sun, the golden triangle that marked his ultimate destination.

She swallowed. "Clay, I'm feeling a little shy. Maybe we should—"

"Shh. Let me look. You're so beautiful, Emily." Her decision to stand on the bumper had accidental benefits he hadn't realized until now. By reaching back to grasp the tailgate, she'd angled her lace-covered breasts forward, and they were at the perfect level.

Heart racing with excitement, he glanced up at her. "Now this is what I call a tailgate party."

Her shallow breathing and flushed cheeks revealed her excitement, even though she frowned at him. "So help me, Clay, if someone shows up I'll kill you."

Holding her gaze, he unfastened the front clasp of her bra. "Want to move into the cab?"

"Yes..." She moaned as he smoothed back the lace and cradled her breasts in both hands. "No...I don't know."

He began a slow massage as he leaned in to kiss her full lips. "When you do, tell me."

Her eager welcome was his answer. She kissed him with enough enthusiasm to make him dizzy. Desire pulsed through him with such urgency that he fantasized spreading the blanket on the ground, unfastening his jeans and taking her.

Gasping and fighting for control, he drew back and looked into green eyes wild with passion. "Damn, Emily."

She gulped for air. "We should stop."

"I know." He brushed her rock-hard nipples with his thumbs. "I can't." He kissed her again, thrusting his tongue deep as his cock strained against the fly of his jeans.

She groaned and pushed her breasts against his palms, reminding him that she had other delights he'd promised himself. He never expected to have this chance again, and he didn't want to miss anything. Reluctantly leaving the pleasure of her hot mouth, he kissed his way down to her breasts.

"I want you," she said, her voice breathless. "I want you so much."

He circled her nipple with his tongue. "I know."

"Are you sure..." She panted as he tugged on her nipple with his teeth. "You really don't have any..."

"No." He licked a path over to her other breast.

She groaned again. "I need you."

"I'm here." Still teasing her quivering breasts with

his mouth, he reached between her damp thighs. She couldn't have his cock, but she could have this. As he pushed his fingers in deep, she tightened around him in response.

Aching with needs he couldn't satisfy, he stroked her steadily. The liquid sound mimicked the rhythmic beat of mating, and yet it wasn't. She was so wet, so responsive, so perfect. And he'd never know the joy of sliding into that pulsing channel. He'd never join with her in the way a man was meant to unite with a woman.

Her soft cries grew faster and more desperate, and he increased the pace. As she came, her contractions squeezed his fingers and her warmth bathed them in the sweet nectar of release. He stifled a groan of frustration.

He'd spent a good part of his life wanting what he couldn't have. Now it seemed he'd have to add Emily Sterling to the list.

THE MOST INTENSE ORGASM of Emily's life was followed by boneless languor, and she gratefully accepted the help of Clay's strong arms as he eased her down from her precarious perch and carried her around to the passenger side of the truck. She felt like a rag doll as he leaned into the cab and deposited her carefully on the seat.

Moments later he was back with the blanket, but she couldn't imagine wrapping herself in it while she was still glowing like an ember. She tucked the blanket beside her tilted head and against the seat, and looked out the windshield at the trees that surrounded the front part of the truck. Clay had pulled it partway into the forest, probably to shade the cab.

The back, however, had been open to the meadow, and that's where she'd chosen to let Clay give her an orgasm. Now that she'd done it, she wondered if that explained why the experience had been so intense. She'd never allowed herself that kind of sexual adventure in the great outdoors.

Clay opened the driver's side door and climbed in. He had her panties in one hand, and he draped them over the steering wheel before turning toward her. "You okay?"

She surveyed his extremely handsome and remarkably pulled-together look. He'd put on his hat, fastened the snaps of his Western shirt and tucked his shirttail into his jeans. She, on the other hand, was sitting here with the hairstyle from hell and wearing absolutely nothing, not even a hat.

Oh, wait. Her bra still dangled loosely from her shoulders. "I'm fine," she said, "but I must look like something the cat dragged in."

"No cat I've ever known has dragged in anything so beautiful."

His compliment warmed her. In fact, everything about this man, from his deep voice to his thrilling touch, made her feel treasured. "Thanks, Clay. That means a lot coming from you."

"Why?"

"I don't think there's an insincere bone in your body. You say what you mean and mean what you say."

"I sure try to."

"And for the record, you delivered on your promise." She looked into his dark eyes. "I will never, ever forget what just happened."

He turned sideways in the seat and reached over to cup her cheek. "Me neither." Tipping his hat back, he leaned across the console and gave her a gentle kiss. Passion hovered in the background of that kiss, lending a rich undercurrent to the sweetness of the gesture.

She sensed that if she held his head and demanded more, he'd give it. Then they'd land right back where they'd been moments ago, mindless with the force of their need for each other. They'd already created problems for themselves. No point in making things tougher.

Gradually he released her and settled back in his seat. "I hope you're not disappointed, but we'll have to skip visiting the sacred site today."

She almost laughed. As if she gave a flip about that after what they'd shared instead. "I'm not disappointed."

He glanced at her and smiled. "Good."

"In any sense of the word."

"Even better." He held her gaze. "We can stay here as long as you like, but eventually we have to go back to the ranch house."

"I know." Sitting up, she pulled her bra together and fastened the clasp. Then she reached for her panties hanging on the steering wheel.

His hand closed over hers. "I didn't mean you should rush. These aren't even close to dry."

Just that much contact was enough to send shivers up

her spine. "I should put them on anyway. People might already wonder why we're not back yet." She pulled her hand out from under his and took the panties. They were still damp and she didn't relish putting them on; nevertheless she slipped them over her feet and up to her knees.

"There's a simple explanation for the delay. You wanted to explore the creek and then you fell in. I doubt anybody's paying that much attention to how long we've been out here."

"Maybe not, but I was supposed to be helping you so that you'd be finished in time to take me for a horse-back ride." Holding on to the dashboard with one hand, she lifted her hips so she could drag on the clammy underwear.

"Here, let me." He leaned over, grasped the panties and pulled them up with quick efficiency.

Just as quickly, she was aroused and ready for action. She froze in place as she fought the urge to ask him to reverse the process. Those talented hands of his could give her another mind-blowing orgasm in no time.

"You can sit down now," he said gently.

She swallowed. "I should probably sit on the blanket instead of the seat, if you wouldn't mind unfolding it for me."

"Sure."

Positioning the blanket brought him back in close proximity. As she felt his warm breath on her bare arm and caught his musky scent, she gritted her teeth to keep from begging him to love her some more. He acted so nonchalant about helping her. He must not be feeling the same tension.

"*Now* you can sit down."

"Thanks." She lowered herself onto the blanket and stared out the window as she tried to get her heartbeat back to normal.

"I probably shouldn't tell you this, but I want you so much right now I can't see straight."

She groaned and buried her face in her hands. "No, you shouldn't have told me." Lifting her head, she looked at him, knowing he'd be looking right back. "What are we going to do about this?"

"I have no idea. Spending the next few days being around you and not able to touch you is liable to drive me crazy."

"Ditto."

"I should never have let you give me that blow job."

"I should never have let you touch my hoo-ha."

He stared at her in obvious frustration. Then slowly he began to grin, then to chuckle. Finally he was full-out laughing.

"What's so funny?"

"Us! We're ridiculous! We're consenting adults, and we should be able to have sex with each other if we want to."

"Yes, but as we've said several times, my father would have a fit if he found out. I don't know if he'd be more upset with me or with you, but he would definitely be upset."

"So we'll make sure he doesn't find out. We'll make sure nobody knows."

She shook her head. "Even if that's possible, it's not just about him, it's about you. What if I break your heart?"

His smile never wavered. "Trust me, Emily, if there's one thing I've learned, it's how to guard my heart. This isn't about my heart. It's about a totally different part of my anatomy."

8

EMILY PULLED THE BLANKET around her. "Let me think about it."

That wasn't the answer Clay had hoped for. "Don't think too long." He started the truck and slowly backed it in an arc so he was facing the meadow again. "When are you leaving?"

"Probably Saturday. I made the trip in one day on the way here, but it's close to seventeen hours. I might break it up going back. I'm supposed to be at work Monday, and I don't want to be wiped out."

He put the truck in gear and started back to the graded road. He hadn't given much thought to her decision to drive, but it was a hell of a long way. "Why didn't you fly?"

"I wanted to save a few bucks."

And here he'd thought she was a spendthrift. Instead she might be a beautiful cheapskate. "Yet you have all this money stashed away."

"I do, and you know what? I feel like giving it back to him."

Clay winced. "I wouldn't, if I were you. I don't think his pride could handle that."

"Maybe I could tell him I won the lottery and wanted to share."

"I—"

"No, that's a really bad idea," she said. "Assuming he's already lied to me about where the money's coming from, I don't want to compound that by creating a second lie in order to give it back."

Clay sighed with relief. "Good. Besides, he wouldn't take it, no matter what story you cooked up. I'm sure in his mind he's the parent who's supposed to give to the kid, not the other way around." From the corner of his eye he saw her nod.

"You're right," she said. "But I promise you, if he needs anything as he gets older and doesn't have savings to cover it, I'll find a way to help him."

"So will I. I know how it feels to depend on the kindness, or sometimes the unkindness, of strangers."

She was quiet for several moments. "You don't have to answer this, but I really want to know what it was like."

He thought about taking the fifth because he didn't enjoy talking about those days. But he had just told her that he knew how to guard his heart, so maybe she needed to understand. "You feel like somebody lost in the desert with no water and no shade. You see this oasis, but when you get there, it's a mirage. Eventually you stop believing in the oasis and you learn to survive without water and shade."

"But what about the Last Chance? Isn't that a real oasis?"

"I want to believe it is, and it's the closest thing to a home I've ever had, but I'm still a hired hand. I sleep in the bunkhouse, and I don't own any part of the ranch."

"Emmett thinks of you like a son."

"I know he does." Guilt pricked him. "Which is why he trusts me with you."

"As he should! You would never let any harm come to me."

"No, I wouldn't." He cut the wheels to the left and the truck bounced over a small ditch as he drove onto the dirt road leading back to the ranch. "But I doubt he'd want me fooling around with you, either."

"More for your sake than mine. He doesn't want you falling for a California girl the way he did."

Clay looked over at her. "That might be part of it, but you're still his little girl, and any man with intentions like mine would probably face a loaded shotgun."

"But I'm twenty-seven years old!"

He couldn't help laughing, because her exclamation made her sound no more than five. Without makeup and wrapped in a blanket, she didn't look twenty-seven, either. More like seventeen. But she probably wouldn't appreciate hearing that.

"I don't think it matters what age you are," Clay said. "I hope I'll be a dad someday—I've watched how they behave with their kids, so I can learn something. They may try to treat their sons and daughters the same, but they don't. They're way more protective of those girls."

"I wouldn't know about that." She sounded sad. "My dad wasn't ever around long enough for me to find out if he'd be protective or not."

Instantly he regretted ever bringing up the subject. "I'm sorry. I have a bad habit of thinking nobody's had childhood problems but me."

"If we're comparing, I certainly had it better than you, though. At least I had a mom and a home."

"There was a time I would have given anything for that, but who knows? I might not have ended up on a ranch, and I love that life. It suits me to a T."

"It does."

He felt her gaze on him and turned to see her smiling in a way that made his groin tighten. "You probably shouldn't look at me like that while I'm driving."

"Why not?"

"Because it makes me want to pull over and ravish you."

"Ravish me?" She laughed. "That sounds like fun."

"I guarantee it would be, but you said you had to think about whether you and I should have any more sexual adventures together."

"I do have to think about it. And not because of my dad's disapproval, either. Still, we might want to hold off until after his birthday."

"Which gives us one whole day?"

"And night."

He groaned. "I can't convince you to sneak out of the house tonight and meet me in the barn?"

"No. My dad will only turn sixty once, and I don't want to risk upsetting him on his big day. Either with a discussion about this supposed inheritance, or by carrying on a secret affair with you."

"You're right." He blew out a breath. "You are so damned right. I'm being selfish to even think of it."

"No, you're not. I've thought of it. I've imagined all kinds of scenarios."

"Yeah?" That gave him hope. "Like what?"

"You don't want to hear them while you're driving."

"You are a hard woman." He avoided a rut partly to save the shocks but mostly because bouncing around with an erection was extremely unpleasant. "And you're turning me into a hard man."

"Now that's funny."

"No," he said with feeling. "Believe me, it's not."

LUCK WAS WITH EMILY, AND SHE made it upstairs without anybody seeing her. She'd been given Nick's old room, although according to Sarah none of the furnishings were the same. Apparently Nick had cherished the bed he'd had in there and had taken it to his house.

Sarah had put a secondhand bed and dresser in the room temporarily while she searched for something more distinctive. Emily hadn't thought much about the room, but as she walked around after a quick shower in the bathroom across the hall, she pictured it with a king-size bed and dresser.

The headboard and footboard of the bed would be made of some kind of rugged wood with old-fashioned brands burned into the surface. The dresser would be constructed the same way, and a red leather armchair in the corner would give the room a splash of color. She liked her vision so much she thought about telling Sarah.

If Sarah had an idea of what she wanted, she might be able to find someone to make it. Emily thought about coming back when everything was done, and how much she'd enjoy sleeping in a room she'd helped design, in a house that she loved. Then she brought herself up short.

What was she doing, turning into some sort of Western girl? One day of hot sex with a cowboy and she'd gone native? How her mother would wrinkle her nose at that.

As if to prove that she was from California and proud of it, she dressed for dinner in a short white skirt and a black tank top. Then she piled on the gold jewelry with big hoop earrings, a three-strand gold necklace and gold bangles on her arm. For good measure she added a gold ankle bracelet and wedge-heeled sandals.

When she walked down the curved staircase to the living room, she found Sarah sitting there drinking wine with a blond woman who looked to be in her late fifties.

"Emily!" Sarah called out. "I wondered if you'd turn up. I have someone I want you to meet."

As Emily walked toward the two women seated in leather armchairs she wondered if, like it or not, she was about to meet her father's girlfriend.

"Hello, Emily." The woman stayed seated but held

out her hand. "I'm Pam Mulholland." She had a warm, firm handshake and kind gray eyes.

Emily wanted to instantly dislike her, but she wasn't the sort of woman to inspire instant dislike. Her dimpled smile of welcome invited Emily to smile back. "I'm glad to meet you. My dad has mentioned you." She didn't add *several times* because that would give more importance to the relationship. At this point, Emily didn't want it to be important.

"And he's certainly mentioned you to me! He's very proud of you."

"That's nice to hear." It was the polite response, but Emily couldn't imagine what her father had to be proud of. She hadn't done much of anything.

She was so focused on Pam that she didn't notice Sarah had left to get another glass from the liquor cabinet until Sarah held it out to her already filled with wine. "Oh! Thank you, Sarah."

"I took a chance that you like red, but please, watch out for that skirt."

"I do like red. Thanks." Obviously she was meant to join them for a little chat. She'd rather not, but she'd taken the wine and now she was caught. She chose a seat next to Sarah. "Is...uh...my dad home yet?"

"Any minute, now," Sarah said. "We're waiting dinner for him, since we sent him off on all those errands to make sure he was gone for the afternoon, we can't very well start dinner without him."

"I should have gone with him," Pam said. "I could have made sure he didn't get sidetracked, but I had so much to do. I'm training the girl who'll take over for me tomorrow night when I come to the party, and she has lots to learn."

"A bed-and-breakfast must be a big responsibility." Emily studied Pam and noted some similarities to her mother—both Pam and Jeri had fair complexions and a nice smile. But Emily's mother had an edge to her, a sharpness that was missing from this woman. Pam definitely seemed softer. She also dressed like a westerner in a yoked shirt and jeans.

"It doesn't seem like a big responsibility to me," Pam said. "But I've been doing it for a while. I suppose it's overwhelming to someone who's just being introduced to the job."

Sarah beamed at her friend. "I'm excited because you're finally getting a whole night off. I don't think you've taken the night off since you bought the place."

"No, I haven't, but Emmett's sixtieth warrants my full attention."

"Indeed." Sarah raised a glass in Pam's direction. "Which reminds me, Emily. How did you and Clay make out at the picnic site?"

Emily was grateful that she hadn't just taken a mouthful of wine, because if she had, it would have spurted all over her white skirt. "Just fine," she said in a voice that sounded almost calm. "The tables and benches are all set up and the fire pits are ready."

"That's great. So here's my plan. We have a yearling named Calamity Sam who's recently developed a phobia about the noise of plastic bags. Gabe keeps meaning to work with him, but he's gone so much with his cutting horse competitions that he hasn't had time. I've asked Emmett to work with Sam tomorrow morning. Desensitizing a horse with a phobia is a tedious job, and it should keep Emmett occupied so we can sneak our nonperishables out to the picnic site."

"And tomorrow afternoon I'm going to develop a plumbing problem at the Bunk and Grub," Pam said. "While he's fixing that, you can haul the perishables out there."

"Can I help in any way?" Emily didn't want her dad's girlfriend to contribute more to the plan than his only daughter.

"Absolutely," Sarah said. "You can be part of the Calamity Sam plan. Two people are usually more effective. While Emmett calms the horse, you can rustle a plastic bag. This may take more than tomorrow's session, but we need to cure that colt of his phobia. I think Emmett will be happy to show off his horse-training skills for you."

"I can do that. After all, I came here to spend time with my dad." She gave that last sentence extra emphasis.

"And he's absolutely thrilled to have you here," Pam said. "So am I, for that matter. I've been eager to meet you after all the wonderful things Emmett has told me about you."

"He has?" Emily had a hard time imagining her dad bragging about her and fought the impulse to ask what those wonderful things had been.

"Of course. He thinks you're so smart, and he envisions great things for you once you settle on a career."

Emily grimaced. A smart dilettante wasn't particularly

admirable. "Finding a career has taken far too long, I'm afraid. You'd think by twenty-seven I'd have more direction in my life, but instead I'm working at something that pays the bills but doesn't really interest me all that much."

"My, my." Pam exchanged an amused glance with Sarah. "Twenty-seven already and you don't know what you want to be when you grow up. Sweetie, I was past fifty before I figured that out."

"As for me," Sarah said, "I married Jonathan and that made the decision for me. I was a rancher's wife. But I chose the man, not the vocation. I didn't realize until after the wedding that I'd made a career choice at the same time. Turns out I love it, but I didn't know I would. Jonathan's first wife wasn't so lucky. She hated ranching and left."

"She did?" Emily had never heard that story. "Like my mother?"

"Not exactly like your mother." Sarah took a sip of her wine. "Diana left her son, Jack, behind. He was only four."

Emily gasped. "She *left* him? How could she do that?"

"I don't know, but Jack had some major problems dealing with his mother's abandonment. Thank God for Josie. She's helped him come to terms with it. I think having a baby is the best thing that could happen to them because Jack can give that kid the security he didn't have."

Emily shook her head in amazement. "And all this time I thought he was your son."

"Well, he is. Just not biologically."

Emily wondered what other important facts she'd missed over the years because she'd visited the ranch under protest and had kept a protective shell around herself the entire time. "I can't imagine what it must have been like for Jack. At least I've known all along that both my parents love me."

"And that's a gift," Pam said. "I can vouch for the fact Emmett loves you dearly. You should see his face light up when he talks about you."

Emily discovered that she couldn't dredge up a single ounce of resentment toward this woman. Pam obviously loved Emmett, and that had to be a good thing. If he couldn't have his daughter around all the time, he should have someone like Pam to brighten his days.

His objection to marrying a wealthy woman seemed silly and old-fashioned. Emily hadn't planned to champion Pam's cause, but now she was inclined to do exactly that. Life could be rough sometimes, and it made no sense to reject love when it was offered.

The front door opened and Emmett came in.

"Speak of the devil." Pam set down her wineglass and stood. "Hey, stranger! Did you get lost in the feed store?" She started toward him.

"I did not. But Ronald's jacked up the price on that watering trough you wanted, Sarah."

"I hope you got it anyway."

"I did, but it took forever. I looked for one with a small dent in it, but then I had to haggle with him for thirty minutes before he knocked a few dollars off."

If offer card is missing write to: The Reader Service, P.O. Box 1867, Buffalo NY 14240-1867 or visit www.ReaderService.com

BUSINESS REPLY MAIL

FIRST-CLASS MAIL   PERMIT NO. 717   BUFFALO, NY

POSTAGE WILL BE PAID BY ADDRESSEE

THE READER SERVICE

PO BOX 1867

BUFFALO NY 14240-9952

NO POSTAGE
NECESSARY
IF MAILED
IN THE
UNITED STATES

GET FREE BOOKS and FREE GIFTS
WHEN YOU PLAY THE...

Lucky 7

Just scratch off the silver box with a coin. Then check below to see the gifts you get!

SLOT MACHINE GAME!
YES!
I have scratched off the silver box. Please send me the 2 free Harlequin® Blaze® books and 2 free gifts for which I qualify. I understand I am under no obligation to purchase any books, as explained on the back of this card.

151/351 HDL FESA

FIRST NAME

LAST NAME

ADDRESS

APT.#

CITY

STATE/PROV.

ZIP/POSTAL CODE

7 7 7   **Worth TWO FREE BOOKS plus 2 FREE Mystery Gifts!**

Worth TWO FREE BOOKS!

Worth ONE FREE BOOK!

TRY AGAIN!

Visit us at: www.ReaderService.com

H-B-07/11

Pam chuckled and gave him a kiss on the cheek. "You're a good bargain hunter, Em."

"Thanks." He smiled down at her. "I try."

Emily had thought she might be uncomfortable seeing a woman being affectionate with her dad. But from the way he was looking at Pam, he obviously returned her love—whether he was ready to admit it or not. Emily was happy for him.

Sarah stood. "Now that you're here, we can have dinner. Let's go tell Mary Lou to start serving."

Picking up her wineglass, Emily stood, too. "So who will be here for dinner?" She vaguely remembered the evening meal as a boisterous affair with all the Chance boys in attendance. But so much had changed since her last visit.

"Just us," Sarah said. "Now that the boys are all married with homes of their own, we've designated Friday as family dinner night. The other nights, sometimes it's just me and Mary Lou." Carrying her wineglass, she headed for the hallway that led to both dining rooms— the large one used at lunchtime and the intimate one for gatherings of family and close friends.

Pam fell into step beside Sarah, leaving Emily to walk with her dad. Emily was impressed with that small gesture, that showed more than words could that Pam wasn't the possessive type.

"And we've also had Alex the past few months," Pam said. "He's been a regular up until recently."

"You're right. Can't forget Alex." Sarah glanced over her shoulder at Emily. "I don't think you've met Alex, but he's Josie's brother and our marketing director. He flew to Casablanca last week to meet his girlfriend, Tyler."

"Casablanca! How exotic."

"Tyler works on a cruise ship," Sarah said.

"But maybe not for much longer," Pam said as they all continued down the hall. "Have you heard anything from him?"

"Not yet, although he might have called Josie. In any case, I predict we'll be planning another wedding soon. I should probably hang out my wedding planner shingle, at the rate we're going."

Pam laughed. "You know you wouldn't want to do it for strangers."

"No, I wouldn't. But for family and extended family, it's fun. I love having young people around."

"So is Clay coming to dinner?" The minute Emily asked the question, she wished she could take it back. Clay had told her himself that he was just a ranch hand. He might fall into Sarah's category of *young people*, but so would many of the hands, and they all ate in the bunkhouse.

Sarah paused and turned back toward Emily. "I hadn't planned on it, but I could call down to the bunkhouse and see if he'd like to come up. I hadn't thought about the fact you might appreciate having someone your own age at the table."

Pam had also turned to face Emily. "Good point. Poor Emily will probably be bored stiff listening to the old folks all evening."

"No, no, that's not true!" Emily hoped she wasn't blushing and was afraid she was. "I'm perfectly happy with present company. I forgot that Clay would naturally eat down there and not up here. Obviously I'm not used to ranch routine. Forget I brought it up."

Sarah gave her a long look. "You're sure? Because he's welcome at the table and it would only take a phone call. We have a direct line to the bunkhouse."

"I'm absolutely sure." Emily linked her arm through her father's. "I'm here to hang out with my dad. It's been a long time since we've had dinner together."

"Too long," Emmett said.

Emily decided to start her campaign right now. "Even better, I'll have a chance to hang out with Pam, too. And just so you know, Dad, I think she's terrific."

Pam smiled at her. "What a nice thing to say. The feeling's mutual."

"Then let's get this mutual admiration society into the dining room." Sarah started down the hall again. "I'm starving."

"Me, too." Pam fell into step beside her.

Emmett didn't move immediately, and because Emily had linked her arm through his, she either had to wait until he did or urge him to get going. She waited, but she had a feeling she knew why he'd hung back.

Sure enough, he fixed her with a father-knows-best look. "I hope you're not getting interested in Clay."

"Of course not, Dad." Good thing noses didn't really grow when a person told a fib.

"He's really attached to this ranch, and we both know you're not into ranch life."

She was beginning to question the truth of that, and whether she really disliked ranches or she'd been

conditioned to dislike them by her mother. But she nodded, because now wasn't the time to discuss it. He might
think she was only saying it to justify her interest in
Clay.

"Exactly. I'm a California girl," she said.

"And a beautiful one, at that. You looked cute in your
jeans and boots, but this is the real you, Emily."

"I suppose." She'd have to find a way to wash out
those jeans so she could wear them again tomorrow.

"I don't have to tell you why I feel so strongly on the
subject."

"No, you don't. I get it."

"It's not just my own history, but Clay's. He may
pretend to be tough emotionally, but his first eighteen
years were rootless. That had to take its toll."

"I'm sure it did. Don't worry, Dad. I understand."

"Good. Now let's go eat."

Her heart was pounding by the time they set off down
the hall again. She hadn't come here to cause problems,
but she was causing them, all the same. She'd slipped
up just now by asking about Clay. He seemed to think
they could carry on right under everyone's nose without
getting caught, but so far she wasn't demonstrating any
talent for subterfuge.

There were a bunch of reasons why she had no business even trying to conduct an affair with Clay. She
needed to tell him that staying away from each other
was the best option. But that didn't mean she had to
like it.

9

CLAY WAITED UNTIL THE bunkhouse was dark and the hands were all snoring before he slipped outside. Hard work and fresh air guaranteed that the guys always slept like the dead. Usually Clay did, too. But tonight there would be no sleep for him until he'd seen Emily.

He figured if they could avoid getting caught, then it didn't matter whether they waited until after Emmett's birthday or not. And they for sure wouldn't get caught tonight. Clay had been sitting around outside talking with the guys before everyone turned in. Emmett had walked past on the way to his cabin and given them a wave.

So Emmett was in for the night, and the ranch house, near as Clay could tell from here, was also dark. He knew which room Emily was in. Somebody, maybe even Emmett, had mentioned that Sarah was giving Emily Nick's old room while she was here.

Clay knew the inside of the house like the back of his hand. Whether the Chances had taken pity on him or whether Nick and Gabe had plain liked him, he'd felt more like a friend to those guys than an employee, and he'd had the run of the place. He knew exactly where Nick's window was on the second story of the west wing.

All the windows had screens on them this time of year, so tossing a pebble at the window wouldn't have the same effect as it would have with glass. Still, he figured enough pebbles tossed would eventually get her attention. Then it would be time to see if she'd go for the next stage; that would take her cooperation and removal of the screen.

Every bedroom on the second floor was equipped with a rope ladder in case of fire. The ladders had been Sarah's idea, according to Nick, and the boys had all embraced the concept with enthusiasm. They'd never needed them to escape a fire, but those ladders had seen plenty of use before the Chance brothers were of legal drinking age.

After that, the boys had used the ladders once in a while for old times' sake, just to keep their comings and goings secret from their folks. Clay was willing to bet a rope ladder was still stored in Nick's closet.

He was planning on it, in fact. All Emily had to do was let down the ladder the way Rapunzel let down her hair in the fairy tale, and...

Well, and nothing, if she'd decided against having sex with him. But he hoped to hell she wanted to, and in case she did, he'd tucked a couple of condoms in his pocket. The scheme was virtually foolproof because nobody else was staying on the second floor in either wing at the moment.

So he was on his way, showered, shaved and dressed in clean clothes. He'd considered whether to wear his hat. Obviously he didn't need one at night, but he sensed the cowboy mystique intrigued her.

He'd worn the hat, and he'd keep it on long enough for her to see him standing below her window looking... cowboylike. Actually, he'd need to keep it on when he climbed the ladder because he didn't relish leaving his precious hat on the ground where anything could happen to it. The hat would be in the way later, but it might serve a seductive purpose in the beginning.

He had a half moon to see by, and his eyes had adjusted to the light enough that he could find his way around to the back of the ranch house without a lot of trouble. He tripped a couple of times on protruding rocks, but only because nerves were making him clumsy. Thank God the Last Chance hadn't installed motion detectors.

Jonathan Chance had hated the things, that he claimed lit up every time a raccoon sauntered by and probably would malfunction if an actual intruder came around. Jonathan had counted on the unpaved road into the ranch to discourage would-be burglars. That and always having at least one dog on the place, although dogs had to be locked in the barn at night because of wolves and coyotes.

Clay heard a pack of coyotes yipping off in the distance as he rounded the end of the house and walked toward Emily's window. No light showed there, either. He wondered if she was asleep.

He stood in the shadows debating whether to wake

her up. She had been up late the night before after driving almost seventeen hours to get here. She deserved a good night's sleep.

But he couldn't assume she was actually sleeping. If today's sexual adventures had left her as hot and bothered as they'd left him, she'd be lying up there drifting on a cloud of ultimate frustration. She might decide to do something about that, even though she was alone.

Clay had considered that option to solve his own problem and had discarded it. He couldn't see going that route unless he struck out completely with Emily. But she might not be thinking that he was standing down here ready to climb a rope ladder to get to her. She might be pleasuring herself right this very minute.

That was enough motivation for him to pick up a small pebble and toss it at her window. It didn't make much noise, so he picked up a slightly larger stone and threw that. When the second stone only rustled lightly against the screen, he went for the next size up. Once again, nerves made him clumsy and he missed the window.

The rock, for that's what it truly was rather than a pebble, hit the side of the house, hard. The loud crack sounded like a well-placed blow from a hammer. Instantly a light flashed on in her room. She appeared at the window and gazed into the darkness.

But as he knew—and she might have to find out— the light made it harder to see into the darkness. It gave him a perfect view of her, however at least from the waist up. In his fantasies about this moment, she'd been wearing a black lace negligee. In reality, she had on a white tank top. With her long blond hair down around her shoulders and her golden tan, she looked very much like a California surfer girl.

But she wasn't in California now, and he didn't really care what she had on. If all went according to plan, she wouldn't be wearing it much longer. As it was, he could tell she wasn't wearing a bra, and that was a good start.

She shrugged and started to turn away from the window. He'd been thinking so intently about the next step that he was neglecting the critical part, getting her to let him in.

The window was open, so she ought to be able to hear him. "Emily," he said in a stage whisper. "Down here."

She whirled back and crouched down to peer through the open bottom half of the double-hung window. "Clay?"

He stepped closer so he could talk more normally. As he gazed upward, he had to smile. Her nose was making a dent in the screen as she pressed forward, trying to see him. "Turn off the light and you can see me better."

She moved away from the window and the light went out. When she came back, she was just a shadowy figure behind the screen. "It is you."

"Yeah." He thought it was a good sign that she didn't ask him why he was there. "Listen, there should be a rope ladder in Nick's closet."

"A *ladder?* What in heaven's name…oh."

"We need to talk." It was the opening line he'd decided on, but he had much more than talking in mind.

She laughed softly. "That's the biggest con in the world and you know it. You don't want to talk."

"Yes, I do."

"Not much, though."

"All right, how's this? I can't sleep knowing you're so close by, so I decided to come over here and check on you. Were you asleep?"

"No."

"Why not?"

"None of your beeswax."

Now it was his turn to laugh. "I have my answer."

"Look, if you were picturing me lying in bed pining for you, then—"

"Actually I was picturing you lying in bed giving yourself a climax and wishing I could be there to do it for you."

Her breath hissed out. "Stop that."

"Will you go look for the ladder?"

"Then what? There's a screen on here."

"You can take that out and pull it inside for now."

"You seem to know all about this process."

"I used to watch Nick do it all the time. Will you go get it?"

"I thought we decided to wait until after my dad's birthday."

"That seems like a waste of a perfectly good night. FYI, your dad is fast asleep in his little cabin. Everyone else on the ranch is also fast asleep. Nobody will ever know that I've been up there."

"Unless they heard you heave that boulder against the side of the house."

"I accidentally missed the window."

"Good thing. You probably would have broken it. That would have been difficult to explain, don't you think?"

He blew out a breath. "Please get the ladder."

"If I do, it doesn't mean anything."

Oh, yes, it does. "All right. I understand."

The light flicked on again and he heard her rummaging around in Nick's closet. After the light went out, she came back to the window. "I found the ladder."

His heart rate picked up considerably. He checked to make sure the condoms were still safely tucked in his pocket. "Just take out the screen. Once you do that, the ladder will hook right over the window sill."

"You know, maybe I should just come downstairs and unlock the front door for you."

"It's not a good idea. The stairs creak quite a bit, and there's always the chance Sarah will hear that, or hear the front door open. She's a parent, and according to her, parents' ears are tuned for that kind of thing. Plus I'd have to leave the same way, and all that running up and down creaky stairs will get us caught for sure."

Emily sighed and started working on the latches holding the screen. "If you say so, but this doesn't seem like the brightest idea in the world, either. This screen is kind of awkward, and I...whoops! Watch out!"

Clay dodged out of the way as the screen came down. Fortunately for anyone below, the frame was made of lightweight aluminum and couldn't do much damage. Unfortunately for the screen, that same aluminum crumpled like paper on impact.

Emily leaned out the window. "You okay?"

"Yep." He picked up the screen. "This thing's a little bent, though." He was thinking more like totaled, but he didn't tell her that.

"Oh, great. You'd better leave while you can. That screen coming down is sure to alert somebody."

"Maybe not. I'll step into the shadows."

"What about the screen?"

"I'll take it with me. We'll figure out some way to explain this if we have to." He was too close to victory to worry about how he'd replace the screen without anybody knowing about it. He stashed the screen behind a bush growing close to the house. Then he counted to one hundred while he waited to see if either Sarah or Mary Lou would sound the alarm.

All quiet. Well, except for the intense pounding of his heart. He moved back to the window. "Let down the ladder."

A few thumping sounds indicated she was hooking it to the windowsill. Then the rope ladder tumbled down in a beautiful cascade. He looked upon it as his personal stairway to heaven.

She leaned out of the window again. "You'd better go slow and test this thing. It looks as if it's been sitting in that closet for years."

"I'm sure. It almost qualifies as an antique. I'm surprised Nick hasn't had it bronzed." He took her advice and balanced on the bottom rung to make sure nothing would give way. The ladder held. "I'm coming up."

"There's something medieval about this, like you should have a sword."

He glanced up. "Sorry. Left my sword at home."

"But I noticed you wore your hat." She sounded amused.

"I feel naked without it."

"Really?"

"Not exactly, but I am used to it. I...damn." As if talking about the hat had been a jinx, a sudden breeze lifted it right off his head. It dropped to the ground, the very ground where he hadn't wanted to leave it.

"Oh, dear." She sighed dramatically. "Now you're naked."

He had a difficult choice. He could go back for the hat and look like a dork who was more concerned about his hat than a rendezvous with a hot woman, or he could leave it and hope a raccoon didn't carry it off. He left the hat.

Another few seconds of climbing, and he pulled himself through the window. It wasn't a graceful entrance, but at least he was now in her bedroom where there was, conveniently, a bed.

She'd backed away from the window to give him room to climb in and stand upright. Once he did that, he felt more in control of the situation. He pulled the ladder back inside and closed the window.

"That means no breeze," she said.

"And no bats."

"Bats?" She put a hand to her chest. "We could have bats in here?"

"You go around leaving windows open with no screens, and you sure could. They're harmless, but there's no point in having one accidentally fly in and scare itself to death."

"Not to mention freaking me out."

"I'd protect you. Besides, like I said, they're not a threat to you."

"Sorry. I grew up in suburbia. Between a bull moose charging me and potential bats in my bedroom, I'm experiencing a little too much *Wild Kingdom* for comfort."

"And that's not even counting the human animal who climbed in your window."

"Exactly." She stood in the shadowed room, her arms crossed over her chest. Besides the tank top, she was wearing boxers in what looked like a plaid design. The combination was somehow sexier to him than a black negligee would have been. Or maybe it was just because Emily was wearing them.

"Actually, I was more worried about the noise than the bats," he said, hoping to calm her fears a little.

"You're assuming there will be noise. I made it clear that allowing you to climb the ladder doesn't mean I've agreed to have sex with you."

"Why not?"

"Because I'm not good at this cloak-and-dagger stuff. When I was walking down the hall to dinner with my dad, Sarah and Pam, I opened my big mouth and asked if you'd be coming to dinner, too."

He could see how that might have attracted some attention, but maybe it wasn't so bad. "That's natural enough. You're not expected to remember who eats where."

"No, but I could have asked if any of the hands were

joining us for dinner. Instead I specifically asked about you, and my dad picked up on it."

A whisper of uneasiness distracted him slightly from his single-minded need to take her to bed. "What did he say?"

"That he hoped I wasn't becoming interested in you because we're from two different worlds, and besides, you had a rough time as a kid. I told him I was not interested in you. Which is, of course, a lie. I think he knew it was a lie, too."

Clay ignored the warning bells in his head. "So tomorrow we'll behave like polite strangers."

"Wouldn't it be a lot easier if we behave that way now, and you go back down the ladder?"

He propped his hands on his hips and gazed at her in the semidarkness. He couldn't see her all that well, but he could hear her breathing, and she wasn't as calm as she'd like him to think. "Is that seriously what you want me to do? Leave?"

"It would make our lives a lot simpler tomorrow."

"Would it, really? I've given this a lot of thought."

She chuckled. "I'm sure you have."

"Oh, and you haven't?"

"Yeah, I have, too. I haven't come up with any answers, either. It's a touchy situation, but I keep thinking if we can keep a lid on it for another twenty-four hours, then—"

"I don't know about you, but I see this like a pressure cooker. If I go back down that ladder right now, the steam builds up and by tomorrow night we might both be ready to blow."

"That's one way to look at it."

If he judged only from her tone of voice, he might believe she was looking at the problem rationally. But there was a breathless undercurrent to her words that told him she might be nearing the breaking point, too.

He decided to press his advantage. "On the other hand, if we let off some of that steam tonight, then we might be able to hang around each other without the same level of tension."

"That's another way to look at it." Her voice quivered ever so slightly.

"Which way do you want to look at it, Emily?"

She cleared her throat. "Did you by chance bring condoms?"

"Two."

"Then maybe we should use them."

It took him only a split second to close the distance between them and sweep her up in his arms.

10

FROM THE MOMENT SHE'D LOOKED out the window to discover Clay standing there, Emily had known it would end up this way, with both of them naked in her bed. Clay had been the image of a determined male, with his legs braced and his shoulders back—a man on a mission. He wanted her and even though she knew they shouldn't, her own hunger was too strong to deny.

She wasn't convinced that his theory of a pressure-cooker made sense, but it meant that she was flat on her back, writhing against the sheets while he kissed every available inch of her. That couldn't be all bad, could it?

"I want to turn on the light, but the curtains aren't heavy enough," he murmured as he brushed his mouth over the very top of her nipple. "Can't attract attention."

"Why do you need the light?" She was proud of herself for managing a complete sentence while he was driving her slowly insane.

"To see your face."

"My face?" She gulped for air as he used his lips and tongue to devastating effect. "What about my naked body?"

"That, too." He traced a path down the valley between her ribs. "But I love how your eyes widen and your pupils get huge when you're excited."

She didn't want to make this *too* easy. "What makes you think I'm excited?"

"Do you usually wiggle around like this?" He dipped his tongue into her navel.

She arched up off the mattress. "All the time. I have an itch."

"Then let me scratch it." And in one swooping motion, he tucked his head between her thighs, slid both hands under her bottom and zeroed in.

She nearly lost what was left of her mind. She wasn't a stranger to this maneuver, but she had to admit Clay's technique topped every experience she'd ever had. For the next several minutes, he owned that territory. If he hadn't thrown her a pillow to muffle her cries, she would have brought the house down as he made her come in a spectacular fashion, and then repeated the fireworks display moments later.

Limp and covered in a sheen of sweat, she was vaguely aware of a condom packet being ripped open, and then he slid into her, smooth and easy, his way paved with two delicious orgasms. He felt so good there that she summoned the energy to rise and meet his second thrust.

An electric impulse rocketed through her at that firm contact, and she knew she wasn't finished yet. Her pelvic muscles tightened without her consciously willing it, and he groaned in response.

She'd recovered enough to remember they had to be quiet. "Shh," she whispered. "Shh."

He pumped again. "But it's so good, Emily. So damned good."

"I know, but we can't make noise." Wrapping her legs around him, she held on and gloried in the way he filled her to the brim. "Kiss me. That will absorb most of the sound."

He covered her mouth with his and began to thrust, long and slow at first, and then faster. She muffled his low, urgent moans and held him close, but not so close that he couldn't move. She needed the urgent rhythm as much as he did, wanted to come…once more…just once…*more*.

With one mighty push, he buried himself deep, his muted cries joining hers as she lifted her hips and shivered in a glorious explosion of pleasure. He shuddered in her arms as the rapid pulsing of his cock teased her womb. She'd never been this susceptible to a man's virility and power. Must be the cowboy in him.

At last he eased his mouth from hers. "Perfect," he murmured. He rocked his hips forward, bringing them even closer together. "Perfect."

"Yes." In the darkness she held him tight and wished this moment never had to end.

CLAY WASN'T SURE HOW MUCH time passed before he roused himself to go across the hall to the bathroom and dispose of the first condom. Yes, he'd brought two, but that didn't mean he had to use both of them. In consideration of his beautiful bedmate, he should probably leave the way he'd arrived and let her rest for whatever hours remained of the night.

Feeling extremely chivalrous, he returned to the room and wondered what the hell he'd done with his clothes. Once she'd agreed to take him into her bed, he'd thrown them every which way, although he'd kept track of the jeans pocket with the all-important condoms. Now, however, he was having a little trouble locating a few key items, such as his briefs and his shirt.

"You're not leaving, are you?"

He glanced toward the bed and could dimly see her propped up on her elbow, gazing at him. "I thought maybe you'd want to sleep," he said.

"You climbed a rope ladder and risked your reputation to make this all happen. Why worry about a silly thing like sleep?"

He abandoned the search for his briefs and walked toward the bed. "I'm not worried about me, but you must be exhausted."

"I'm feeling very, very mellow." She held out a hand to him. "But that's different from being exhausted. Besides, I've never had the pleasure of a totally naked Clay Whitaker. I can't see you without turning on a light, but I can use the Braille method. Come down here so I can explore."

Only a stupid man would refuse an invitation like that. He stretched out on his side next to her. "I'm just your standard-issue male," he said.

"I can testify *that's* not true." She reached down and

took hold of his very happy johnson. "Exhibit A. This particular item is way above average."

He didn't care to know how she was able to judge that. Funny how quickly possessiveness could set in, even when he knew she wouldn't ever commit to him.

"And when you consider the whole package, then you're a bargain at any price." Sliding her hand under his balls, she balanced each one in her palm. "There's nothing standard about you, Whitaker. Everything is supersized."

He loved having her hands on him, but he pretended to take her fondling in stride. "I don't know that it matters all that much."

"It matters." She traced a line up the underside of his penis, that was beginning to show interest in resuming the program. "The added value here increases the friction for me, which is all kinds of good. And these—" She caressed his balls again. "I could feel them brush my skin with each thrust. That's the kind of experience a girl remembers."

"Good to know." Yes, he was definitely going to use that second condom. "Now it's my turn." He ran his knuckles across her breasts. "Kissing you here and having you arch up because you want my mouth all over you is almost enough to make me come."

"That's nice." Her low, sexy voice egged him on.

"And you taste good, too."

"Spearmint toothpaste."

"I meant here." He slid his hand between her thighs and stroked up and in, his fingers creating the sweet music of sex as he moved them slowly back and forth.

She moaned. "That feels…"

"Nice?" He rotated his thumb lightly over her clit.

"More than nice." Her breath caught. "I've never been so…"

"Neither have I." So soon, and he was hard again, throbbing with the need to have her.

"Should we…" She whimpered softly.

He found her G-spot with his middle finger and smiled as she began to pant. "Should we what, Emily?"

"Worry."

"Not now. Right now I'm going to kiss you so you can yell if you want." He angled his mouth over hers and concentrated on that G-spot until she came so lustily that he wondered if she'd bite his tongue in her frenzy. But she didn't. He eased his hand free and caressed her slick thighs. "That was fun."

"Uh-huh." Gasping, she flopped back on the bed. "I mean it, Clay." She gulped for air. "I'm not usually like this."

"I'm not, either."

"From the moment I saw you today with that canister of semen on your shoulder, I wanted to jump you."

He started to laugh and turned his head into the pillow to mute it.

"I suppose that does sound funny, but honest-to-God, you looked so manly."

He cleared his throat. "I never thought of semen collection as a way to get girls."

"I'm sure it's not that. Well, maybe it added to the mystique since you'd just been involved in something sexual and you had the evidence to prove it."

"If all that's true, what's my excuse? Why have I been in a constant state of semiarousal ever since I saw you this morning?" He was in a state of full arousal now, but he could wait.

Once he used the second condom he'd have no reason to stay and risk being discovered here in the morning. And lying in the dark talking was nice. Although sex was never far from his mind when he was with Emily, he just liked being here, sharing the same space.

"You tell me," she said. "I've had boyfriends before, obviously, but I can't imagine any of them climbing a rope ladder in the middle of the night just to have sex with me."

"This is going to sound dorky as hell, but I think it's the long buildup."

"What buildup? We just saw each other this morning."

"Yeah, but apparently I've wanted you for ten years."

"Wow. No wonder you've been talking about pressure cookers. That's a long time to have a boner."

Once again he had to turn his face into the pillow to keep from hooting out loud. "Okay," he said once he could speak again. "It wasn't that bad. It's not like I've thought of you constantly for ten years. That would be pathetic."

"And crazy. I wasn't that memorable."

"Oh, you were damned memorable in your short shorts and low-cut blouses. You may not remember me, but I sure as hell remember you. I flirted with you like crazy."

She was quiet for several seconds. "I sort of remember, and I'll bet I wasn't very nice to you, either. I'd hoped you'd forgotten."

"Nope. But all this sex has taken the sting completely out of it."

"I apologize for being such a jerk back then, Clay. It only shows how stupid I was at that age. What horrible things did I say, if you don't mind me asking?"

"You told me in no uncertain terms that cowboys weren't your type."

She rolled to her side, facing him. "Those were my mother's words and I was dumb enough to parrot them without thinking whether it was true for me. I'm so, so sorry for being mean and rude."

"But cowboys really aren't your type," he said softly. He'd do well to remember that simple fact.

"I don't know." She reached for him, brushing her fingers over his chest. "You're my type, and you're a cowboy."

"Yes, ma'am."

She chuckled. "I like it when you sound like that. Maybe cowboys are my type, after all." She toyed with his nipples.

He drew in a deep breath. If she kept that up, they'd be searching for the second condom very soon. "But the thing about cowboys is that they tend to hang out at ranches. That could be a problem for a surfer girl." He said it lightly, but he hoped she'd heard what he was trying to tell her.

"I guess so." She moved her hand lower and encountered his rock-hard penis. "Oh my goodness."

She wrapped her fingers around it. "What are we doing talking when we could be engaged in something far more stimulating?"

"Beats me." He didn't want to admit he'd been holding off using the last condom because then he'd have to leave. Technically the relationship was supposed to be about sex, but for him it had already gone beyond that. When he'd woken up this morning he'd thought he didn't much care for Emily Whitaker. What a difference a day made.

"It's party time." She rubbed her hand up and down, her touch firm enough to make her intentions clear. "Do you know where your condom is?"

"Yes. Don't stop what you're doing."

"Wouldn't dream of it."

Leaning back, he reached blindly over the side of the bed, located his jeans and pulled them onto the mattress. Once he'd taken out the condom packet, he shoved the jeans to the floor and tore open the wrapper.

"Wait. I want to put it on."

"In the dark?"

"You did."

"I've had lots of practice."

"Let me try. I've always wanted to and never felt I could ask before. It seemed too personal, somehow, and I was worried I'd mess up."

"So you're turning the guy you barely know into a guinea pig?" He was secretly flattered. It meant she felt more comfortable with him than she had with other guys.

"Funny, but it feels like I know you really well."

"You will if you fumble the condom application. All that contact is liable to have an undesired effect, like early liftoff, if you know what I mean." He handed the condom to her and hoped for the best.

"So you can give me instructions."

He groaned. "Just let me do it."

"No. Lie down. It's probably good for you to have somebody else in charge once in a while."

"Fine. You can be in charge of pulling up the ladder after I leave. How's that?"

"Boring. I'm in charge of this. Go on, now. Lie down."

He stretched out on his back and wondered what he could think about that would keep his climax at bay. Not his work, that was for sure. That was all about stallions getting it on. So he'd think about...

"I blew air into it so it would go on easier."

"You did *what*?" He raised up on his elbows and discovered that even in the dim light he could see she'd created a balloon out of the condom. "Tell me, have you *ever* seen a guy do that?"

"No, but it seemed logical. Men aren't always logical about these things. Besides, you weren't giving me any instructions, so I had to figure it out for myself."

"Let the air out."

"Okay. But I'll bet it will slide right on now that it's all expanded."

"Not really. That's why you're supposed to roll them on gradually. It's not like putting on a sock."

"Oh! It's like putting on nylons. I get it. I'll just scrunch it back up. Okay, I'm ready now. Hold still."

Clay could predict she was going to have trouble with the condom now that she'd handled it so much, and he knew the solution but was afraid to suggest it. Anticipation had him balancing on the very edge of an impending orgasm.

Sure enough, the condom didn't want to simply slide on the way it would have fresh out of the package. The more she struggled, effectively massaging the sensitive tip of his johnson, the more his control faded.

She made an impatient noise. "I can't seem to make it cooperate."

He couldn't see an alternative. He'd just have to be strong. "If you get the surface wet, it should go on easier."

"Oh. Oh! I should have thought of that." And she began to lick.

He clenched his teeth together and thought about the most boring job in the world, stringing fence. It didn't help. "That's enough," he muttered.

"I don't think so." She took all of him into her mouth.

"Emily!"

Slowly she released him. "I want to make sure you're wet enough."

A hint of laughter in her voice told him she knew he was in bad shape. Of course she'd know. He was breathing like a winded trail horse on an incline. "You're enjoying this, aren't you?"

"Uh-huh."

"Just remember what I warned you about."

"I'm not worried. You're all about discipline and

order. You wouldn't let yourself come. And when you do, after all this torture, it'll be more intense. You'll see."

He dragged in a breath. "That's assuming I live long enough."

"Poor baby. Here you go." She put on the condom, and although it wasn't the most efficient application ever, she accomplished the task. "And since you're already on your back, I'm climbing aboard. After all, you know what they say on the bumper stickers."

"Save a horse, ride a cowboy?"

"Exactly." Positioning a knee on either side of his hips, she poised herself above him. "Ready?"

"I'm beyond ready." He braced himself for the sensation of her slick heat, and still he groaned as she lowered herself, taking him right up to the hilt. It would be so easy to let go, but she was right about him. He was all about self-discipline.

It took every ounce he had to keep from coming as she braced her hands on his shoulders and rode him hard. He bracketed her hips with both hands and urged her on as the blood roared in his ears. He felt her tighten around his cock, and only then did he begin to let loose.

At the moment of her climax, she slowed her movements and kissed him, yet the mouth-to-mouth contact wasn't enough to quiet her deep-throated moans of pleasure as she rocked back and forth. Heat poured through him, demanding release. With one mighty upward thrust, he found it, and his world shattered.

As he whirled in the carnival ride of an incredible

orgasm, he wondered if he'd come back to earth and discover his world was still in pieces. If so, only one woman could put it back together. That made him vulnerable, very vulnerable, indeed.

11

EMILY LONGED TO SPEND the rest of the night wrapped in Clay's strong arms, but that was a risk neither of them could afford. Life began early on the ranch, especially during the summer months, and Clay needed to be back in his bunk long before dawn. So she didn't stop him this time when he came back from the bathroom and started gathering his clothes.

She slipped back into her boxers and tank top, as if to help signal that the rendezvous was over. "Did you hear the plan for tomorrow…I mean today?" she asked as he pulled on his jeans and tucked his shirt into the waistband.

"No. All I know is I have another semen collection in the morning."

"From the same horse?"

"No. Different horse. We don't want to collect Bandit's semen too often because that lowers the value." He sat on the edge of the bed to put on his boots.

"Darn it. I wanted to watch that process, but I'm

supposed to help Dad work with Calamity Sam on the plastic bag thing."

"They're making Emmett do that on his birthday?"

"It's a tactic, so he won't notice all the nonperishables being trucked out to the picnic site."

"Oh." He stood. "Usually with a desensitizing session, the horse gets a break now and then to run around the corral and let off steam. You might be able to come over and watch the collection process during one of those breaks."

"I'd like that. I have to admit I'm fascinated. How do you get the stallion...excited?"

His smile flashed in the dim light. "I can only imagine what you're picturing. And some people actually do use manual stimulation."

"Oh my God."

"It's strictly a clinical process."

"Yeah, right."

"It is, I swear. This is business, like milking a cow."

She laughed. "I don't *think* so."

"Well, anyway, I prefer using a teaser mare."

"So how does that work? Do you dress her up in fishnet stockings and a bustier?"

"We only did that once, and nobody thought to take pictures."

She stared at him. "You're not serious."

"No." He smiled and reached for her, drawing her into his arms. "Unlike the human male, all a stallion needs is a whiff of a mare in season, and he's ready to roll. We just have to make sure he never gets to her."

She nestled against him, relishing the solid feel of his body. "You intercept the goods, in other words."

"Yes, ma'am, that's exactly right." He massaged the small of her back.

"I think I've figured out what an AV is, too, and it's not an artificial vacuum, is it?"

"It didn't seem like the sort of subject you wanted to discuss with your dad, so I made that up."

"Instead it's an artificial hoo-ha, right?"

"Yes."

"Clay, do you think I could watch? I've heard about artificial insemination. Who hasn't? And the insemination part was never a mystery. But I never thought about how the semen was collected. For animals, I mean. I know perfectly well how sperm banks operate."

"This is...different."

"I can tell! And when you're working with such a large animal, the logistics boggle my mind."

"Tell you what. I'll stop by the corral and let you know when it'll happen. Oh, and if I carry the canister out on my shoulder again, does that mean you'll be hot for me tomorrow night, too?"

She looped her arms around his neck. "After what happened here tonight, you won't even need the canister, cowboy."

"That's good to know, but I'll probably saunter by the corral with it on my shoulder, just for good measure."

"I'll look forward to that." She stood on her tiptoes, sliding her body against his, and kissed him lightly on the mouth. "You should get going."

"I know. But I need one for the road." He lowered his head.

His kiss was so thorough that she was achy again when he finished. "No fair. How am I supposed to sleep after that?"

"You're not." He kissed the tip of her nose. "You're supposed to lie here and miss me. You're supposed to miss me so much that you can hardly wait until I'm back in your bed tomorrow night after the party. Back in your bed and deep inside your sweet—"

"How about you?" She rubbed her pelvis over his crotch. "Will you be lying awake missing me?"

"What do you think?"

Reaching down, she caressed the bulge pushing against his fly. "I think you will."

"I will." After one quick, hard kiss, he walked over to the window and raised it. Then he leaned down, picked up the ladder and hooked it to the sill before letting it drop. "Here's hoping my hat's still down there. I don't see it, but it could be there in the shadows."

"Do you only have one?"

"No, I have another one, but that's my best hat, and I'm partial to it."

"Then I hope it's there." Emily held on to the top part of the ladder as Clay climbed out of the window and started down.

When his face was even with hers, he leaned forward. "One more."

She kissed him quickly. "That's all. You're making me nervous."

"It'll be fine. See you in the morning, sweet cheeks." With a cocky grin, he climbed to the ground.

She started pulling the ladder up, but paused when she heard him swear softly. "What's the matter?"

"Can't find my damned hat."

"You need a flashlight."

"I know, but I don't dare get one and prowl around with it. Someone might think I'm a burglar."

She peered downward. "What color is it?"

"Brown. Which doesn't help much in the dark."

"I can't see anything from here, either."

He glanced up at her. "Go ahead and pull the ladder up and close the window. If I don't find it soon, I'll come back tomorrow and look for it."

"Okay. Night." As she finished pulling up the ladder, he continued to search. She kept hoping to hear him call out that he'd found it. When he didn't, she closed the window. She sure as hell didn't want to add a bat to the night's excitement.

On the other hand, she was having more fun than she'd had in a long time, and that wasn't even counting all the great sex with Clay. She tried to picture her mother riding out to the picnic site in an old truck and helping to dig fire pits. Jeri would be worried about ruining her manicure.

Emily hadn't thought about her manicure once today, and she wasn't about to turn on a light and look at it now. No, she would stretch out on this lovely bed that still held Clay's scent and relive the time they'd spent together there. She'd think about the fun they'd had today and how quickly the time passed when she was with him.

All that added up to more than a purely sexual affair, and she doubted he believed that's what they were having, either. She really liked Clay, liked him more than maybe any guy she'd dated. She wasn't sure if she liked cowboys in general or this particular one, but the boots and hat were part of who he was, and she was into it.

Her mother was right about the life of a rancher, though. Emily wasn't sure how she'd feel about spending all her days working outside and dealing with animals, both domestic and wild. Besides that, there wasn't a beach even remotely close to Jackson Hole. Lakes, yes, but lake surfing just hadn't caught on for some reason.

Surfing was her ultimate stress-buster. Catching a wave required split-second timing, and once she was up, the rush of riding that wave swept away all her worries. Californians loved their therapy, but she thought surfing beat sessions on the couch any day.

On the other hand, the beach where she loved to surf had nary a cowboy on it, let alone someone as yummy as Clay. Her dad had once told her that life was about choices, and for every choice you make, there's something else you're giving up. She'd never thought about that statement much until now.

She must have been more tired than she thought, because in spite of desperately wanting Clay beside her, she drifted off to sleep. She dreamed of a cowboy riding a surfboard wearing a brown Stetson. She woke up to sunshine and the fervent hope that Clay had found his hat.

CLAY DIDN'T FIND HIS HAT, not that night, and not early in the morning when he gave the guys some lame excuse for why he needed to go wandering over behind the ranch house. Worse yet, the mangled screen he'd shoved behind the bushes was also gone. He could blame the missing hat on raccoons. They loved carrying things off, for some reason.

But he couldn't picture a raccoon carting off that screen. It was too big and not the sort of thing they'd be willing to drag to their den. Someone had found it, and now he had to sweat out who it might be and whether they'd draw any conclusions about why a screen that had obviously fallen from Emily's window was tucked into the bushes.

He reminded himself that nobody knew how close he and Emily had become yesterday. But she had opened her mouth last night about inviting him to the family dinner table. That could be a tip-off. All he could do was go about his business and see how everything played out.

Breakfast at the bunkhouse had been a raucous affair because it seemed Watkins hadn't slept in his bunk last night, either. It was a testament to how preoccupied Clay had been that he hadn't noticed that Watkins left the bunkhouse late in the evening and never came back, not even for breakfast.

Everyone speculated that Watkins had finally talked his way back into Mary Lou's bed, but if he'd struck out, he might have been too embarrassed to come back and had spent the night under the stars. Clay was glad Watkins's love life provided such a distraction.

If he could be lucky enough to have Watkins find his hat, things might be okay. Watkins would just return it without asking questions.

After breakfast down at the bunkhouse, Clay put on the hat he'd worn the day before, the one he didn't mind sweating in. The brown Stetson had been his dress hat, and he'd been a vain fool to wear it in an attempt to impress Emily. No hat at all would have been the smart choice.

He wondered what would have happened if he'd shown up under her window with no hat. Would she still have agreed to let him climb that ladder? He'd never know, but he'd gone all out in an attempt to get into her bed, and for all he knew, his good brown hat had tipped the balance in his favor. But he wished it hadn't gone missing.

He'd taken Patches, a brown-and-white paint scheduled for collection this morning, to the wash rack. As he hosed down the horse, Emmett walked by and Clay called out a birthday greeting. He'd bought the foreman a new pair of work gloves, really nice leather ones, but he wouldn't bring those out until tonight's party.

Emmett raised a hand in greeting. "Thanks!" he called, as he continued toward the ranch house.

Clay shouldn't assign any special meaning to the fact Emmett hadn't stopped for a chat. His daughter was at the house, and they had a project planned for this morning. Emmett must be going to get her and didn't want to waste time.

Clay understood that. But if he'd stopped for a word or two, even about the weather—which continued to be hot for Jackson Hole—then Clay could have gauged whether there was anything different about Emmett's attitude toward him.

As it was, Clay had to comfort himself with the thought that if Emmett had found that brown hat under Emily's window, he would have raised holy hell about it. Emmett had been the foreman when the Chance boys used those ladders to sneak out at night for keggers in the meadow. He had to know about those fire ladders. Clay tried to calm the churning in his gut.

From the wash rack, Clay saw Nick's truck pull into the circular gravel drive in front of the ranch house. Dominique got out and walked up the steps to the house, while Nick headed over to join Clay.

"Big doings today," Nick said as he approached. "Dominique came over with me so she could help Sarah get some of the supplies out there this morning. We, of course, are supposed to carry on as if nothing is different."

Clay wondered what Nick would think if he knew how absolutely different everything was today, at least for two people on this ranch. "I think Emmett suspects something's going on with his birthday. It's hard to put anything over on him." And although Clay didn't regret a single second he'd spent with Emily, he'd been ignoring that salient point the whole time.

"He probably does suspect something. Oh, well." Nick glanced over at Patches. "Don't you suppose that's enough hose time on his rump?"

"Absolutely!" Clay turned the spray on the horse's withers. He'd been caught daydreaming and paying no attention to his job. That was likely to draw attention because he wasn't known as a woolgatherer.

"Have you washed his penis and foreskin?"

"Yep." Clay had taken care of that first thing, because he had a feeling he'd be absentminded today between his lack of sleep and his preoccupation with Emily.

"Then I'll go fetch Cookies and Cream so we can get this show on the road." He started in through the back door of the barn.

"Uh, Nick?"

He turned. "Yeah?"

"Any objection if Emily pokes her head in during the procedure? She wants to see how this works."

"I don't care, as long as she's quiet and doesn't distract Patches. But…did Emmett make a special request to let her watch?"

"No, why?"

Nick pushed back the brim of his hat and stuck his thumbs in his belt loops. "Well, because I thought we didn't much like her, Clay."

"I know that's how everybody feels, but—"

"I mean, she's taking Emmett's money and has the gall to sneer at how he makes it. So I'm confused as to why we should accommodate her request unless Emmett wants us to."

Clay wasn't prepared for his visceral response to having someone attack Emily. His words came out harsher than he'd meant them to. "She's not like that."

"Oh, really? What makes you think so?"

In the afterglow of last night's lovemaking, Clay had forgotten that everyone on the ranch, with the exception of Emmett and now himself, thought Emily was an ungrateful brat. But Clay wasn't at liberty to talk about the inheritance lie Emmett had been telling his daughter, or even that she'd saved every penny Emmett had sent her.

He thought about what he could say without betraying her trust. "I spent some time with her yesterday, and I just think we might be misjudging her."

Nick studied him. "I see."

"Look, I'm just saying—"

"Am I remembering right that you had a major crush on her the summer you came to live here and she visited for a week or so?"

Clay shrugged. "I might have. Don't remember for sure."

"I do." Nick pointed a finger at him. "And you did. She was sashaying around in those Daisy Dukes and your tongue was dragging in the dust."

"Your memory is better than mine, then."

Nick gazed at him, his expression thoughtful. "She can watch, I guess. But be careful, buddy. According to all I've heard, she's a scheming little—"

"No, she's not. I've talked to her, and she's not like that."

"If you say so. I'm reserving judgment. Once she stops accepting those checks, I might be convinced that she's a nice person, but from where I sit, she's taking advantage of a guy I happen to care about, and that doesn't sit well with me."

"Nobody's forcing Emmett to mail those checks."

"No, but all Emily has to do is bat those big green

eyes at him and whine about how much she's missed having a father around. She plays on his guilt and he writes checks. Simple as that. Oh, and you're creating quite a mud puddle there. I think Patches is clean enough."

As Nick headed into the barn, Clay turned off the hose and swore under his breath. That had not gone well. When Emily made her innocent request to watch the semen collection process, she'd probably also forgotten that she wasn't a popular visitor around here.

Clay hated that for her because she didn't deserve such a bad reputation. But he'd promised to keep their conversation to himself, and that meant he was helpless to protect her from any snubs that might come her way. He understood why she didn't want to confront Emmett today, on his sixtieth. But tabling that discussion would make her life a lot tougher.

Damn, he wished he knew where his hat was.

12

EMILY COULD HAVE WAITED for her dad in the living room, but Sarah and Dominique were in there making lists of supplies to take out to the picnic site. So she figured she had a better chance of catching a moment alone with her father if she stayed in the kitchen.

Mary Lou was busy, as usual, and kept going back and forth from the kitchen to her apartment, which was adjacent to it. At one point Emily thought she heard a male voice in there, but it could have been the TV. Maybe Mary Lou had a show she liked to watch while she attended to her morning duties.

So Emily sat in the kitchen drinking coffee, a wrapped present at her elbow, and waited for Emmett to show up. She hadn't celebrated a birthday with her dad in ten years, and she regretted that. He hadn't celebrated her birthday with her very often, either, come to think of it.

Her birthday was February first, and traveling to Jackson Hole in the middle of winter had made no sense—especially since she'd never developed an interest in winter sports. Her dad had made it to Santa Barbara twice for her birthday. Once when she was six and when she turned twelve.

Both occasions had been awkward because he didn't fit into her suburban lifestyle. He'd stayed in a motel and had come over for the parties; they had involved a jumping castle when she was six and a gaggle of girls going to the movies when she was twelve. Emily had ended up hoping he wouldn't come for her birthday anymore.

What a shame that they couldn't have found more middle ground. But at least she was here today and could wish him a happy birthday first thing in the morning. And give him one of her presents, because she believed birthdays should involve presents all day long.

He walked in, smiling and looking very dashing in his blue striped Western shirt and worn jeans. He was holding his hat. Even though cowboys sometimes kept their hats on indoors, her dad was old school about that and always took his off.

He'd aged well, she thought with pride. He was still lean, and his dark hair, though graying, was as thick as ever. The mustache he'd had ever since she could remember suited him perfectly.

She jumped up and hurried over to give him a kiss on the cheek. His pine-scented shaving lotion was achingly familiar. "Happy birthday, Dad."

"Thanks, Em." His smile remained, but there was a look in his blue eyes she couldn't quite place. She wondered if he worried about growing older. Birthdays affected people differently. Some people loved marking the passage of years and others didn't. Sad to say, she didn't know into which category he fell.

"Here's your first present." She grabbed her package off the table. She'd found wrapping paper with horses on it and was very proud of that. Although she could make fancy bows, she'd tied a simple green ribbon around the package because she didn't want her dad to think it was too frilly and fussy.

"Why, thank you."

"Here's the man of the day!" Mary Lou bustled into the kitchen. "Can I pour the birthday boy some hot coffee?"

"Half a cup," Emmett said. "I'll sit down a minute and open my present. But then Emily and I have to get down to the corral. Oh, and we'll need a plastic bag, Mary Lou, if you have one handy."

Mary Lou poured a mug full of coffee, ignoring Emmett's suggestion of only half, and handed it to him. "Here you go."

"Thanks." He took it without commenting on the extra portion and took a sip. "You make great coffee, Mary Lou."

"And you've never been satisfied with half a cup, so you might as well stop telling me that's what you want. Now open your present. Let's see what Emily brought you."

Emily ducked her head to hide her smile. Not many people got away with bossing her father around, but Mary Lou had been on the ranch about as long as Emmett and obviously wasn't intimidated by any man, let alone her dad.

"I believe I will." Emmett sat down at the kitchen table that served as a gathering place for anyone wanting coffee and conversation during the day. After setting his mug and hat on the table, he carefully untied the green ribbon.

To Emily's surprise, she was nervous about whether he'd like her gift. Because she didn't spend much time with her dad, she wasn't sure what he might want. She'd also been feeling a little sentimental when she'd decided on this one.

After untying the ribbon, Emmett wound it up and set it on the table before peeling off the tape. His care in unwrapping her gift brought a lump to her throat. She'd sent him presents over the years, but too often she'd treated it as an obligation to get out of the way. Now she realized he must have devoted this much attention to opening each one, and she wished she'd put more thought into her other gifts.

Mary Lou blew out an impatient breath. "You are *the* slowest present opener in the whole world, Emmett Sterling."

Emmett glanced up at her. "If someone takes the time to buy me a present and wrap it, I like to appreciate the effort."

"Then I'm going to tell everyone coming tonight to bring their presents in a paper sack. Otherwise we'll be there till dawn while you open them."

"What's this about presents in paper sacks?" Watkins sauntered out of Mary Lou's apartment. His hair and handlebar mustache were still slightly damp, as if he'd recently shaved and showered.

Emmett's eyebrows lifted as he gazed at Watkins. "Morning, Watkins."

"Same to you, Emmett. And happy birthday."

"Thanks." Emmett continued to stare at the ranch hand. "Sleep well?"

"I surely did. And you?"

Emily watched the two men, fascinated by what wasn't being said. Obviously Watkins had spent the night with Mary Lou and that had been the male voice Emily had heard a few minutes ago. If Emily had to guess from her dad's reaction, that wasn't part of the normal routine.

"Oh, for heaven's sake!" Mary Lou stepped forward and handed Watkins a mug of coffee. "Stop dancing around the issue, both of you. Watkins and I spent the night together, Emmett. If he behaves himself, we may continue to do that now and then. I told Sarah and she's fine with it."

Emmett took a sip of his coffee. "And I never said I wasn't."

"No, but you should have seen the look on your face when Watkins walked out of my apartment."

"I was surprised, is all."

"You shouldn't be. Watkins has been sweet on me for years."

"And she finally took pity on me," Watkins said. "I promise you, Emmett, that it won't interfere with my work."

"I wouldn't expect it to," Emmett said.

Emily could hardly wait for a moment alone with Clay so she could tell him about this. She and Clay weren't the only ones who'd enjoyed a rendezvous last night. They might not have to worry about Mary Lou interfering with their plans for tonight, either.

"And that's enough on that topic," Mary Lou said. "Are you finally going to finish opening that present, or do you need someone to do it for you?"

"I've got it." Emmett folded back the wrapping paper and picked up a framed five-by-seven picture. Emily had found the snapshot when she was going through some old boxes. The original was faded and bent, but she'd taken it to a shop where they'd created a new and improved version.

Fifteen years ago, she'd had one of the ranch hands take the picture with her camera when she'd spent a week at the ranch. She and her dad were both sitting on horses, and at twelve she'd insisted on wearing sandals, shorts, a halter top and sunglasses. Definitely no cowgirl.

In the picture, her dad looked like the quintessential cowboy. And even though she winced now to think of how stubborn she'd been about proper riding attire, she still loved this picture. She hoped he did, too.

Mary Lou came over to take a look. "Oh, now that's sweet. Don't you think so, Watkins?"

The barrel-chested cowboy walked over to check out the picture. "Very nice. I think I remember when that was taken."

Emily appreciated their comments, but the man she needed to hear from hadn't said a word. Maybe she'd made a terrible mistake and he'd just shove it in a drawer. He might not care about an old picture like this, after all.

"You don't have to keep it if you don't want to, Dad," she said.

"Of course I'll keep it." His voice sounded rusty and he coughed. "Thank you, Emily. I thought I'd never see this again."

"I wondered if you still had a copy somewhere."

"I used to. Kept meaning to frame it and never did. Had it propped against a lamp beside my bed for the longest time, and then one morning I had it in my hand while I was drinking coffee and walking around the cabin, which wasn't very smart of me. I tripped and doused it with coffee. Ruined it."

Emily sighed with relief. "I was afraid you didn't like it." Instead he'd loved it more than she had. "I made a new copy for myself, too."

"Good." Emmett blinked and cleared his throat. He still hadn't looked at her.

She understood. A man like Emmett would be embarrassed to let anyone know that he could get misty-eyed and choked up over a simple picture. "I guess we need to get down to the corral, though." Until her dad was thoroughly absorbed in the Calamity Sam project, Sarah and Dominique couldn't begin ferrying supplies out to the picnic site.

"Yes, we do." Emmett polished off his coffee in several long gulps. The man had to have a cast iron throat. Then he folded the wrapping paper back around the picture and laid the ribbon on top before picking up everything along with his hat. "You can meet me down at the corral, Em. I'm going to run this home so nothing happens to it."

Emily hadn't thought about what he'd do with the picture once he'd unwrapped it. "I could put it in my room for the day, if you want."

"Nope. This is special and I'd rather make sure it's safe and sound in my house. Finish your coffee and get that plastic bag from Mary Lou before you come down. I'll see you in a few minutes."

Watkins had ducked back into Mary Lou's apartment and returned clutching his hat. "I'll walk out with you, Emmett." He gave Mary Lou a quick kiss. "Thanks, Lou-Lou." Then he followed Emmett out of the kitchen.

After the two men left, Mary Lou let out a sigh. "I hope I'm not going to regret letting that cowboy back into my bed. I should have known he'd make a grand entrance to solidify his position."

Emily was gratified that Mary Lou would share such a personal statement with her. It made her feel more a part of ranch life. "Sounds like he really likes you, though."

"He does, but I've been sleeping solo for a lot of years. And I've warned him not to bring up marriage like he did last time."

"You don't want to get married?"

"No, I don't. At my age, there's no point to it. It's not like we have to worry about which last name to give the kids."

"I see what you mean."

Mary Lou smiled at Emily. "That picture was a

brainstorm on your part. Did you see how emotional he got over it?"

"Yeah." Emily smiled back. "That was nice. I think I need to be around for his birthday every year."

"He pretends like he doesn't want a fuss made over him, but I know he'd love that."

"He would." Emily's heart squeezed as she thought of all the birthdays her dad had celebrated without her. "As a matter of fact, so would I."

As CLAY CAME OUT OF THE BARN leading a well-scrubbed Patches, Emily bounded down the ranch house steps, a plastic bag in one hand. Dear God, she was gorgeous. Her blond hair shimmered in the sun, making her look angelic. He knew she wasn't, but he was struck speechless by the sight of her.

Once again she was dressed in shorts and a scoop-necked T-shirt. She carried the hat she'd borrowed from Sarah in her other hand and put it on once she'd cleared the steps. He wondered if she'd find a way to get her jeans washed for the ride to the picnic site tonight. She wouldn't want to make that ride in shorts.

She spotted him and waved. Because she was coming in his direction, he waited for her. Nick was already in the shed with Cookies and Cream, so he couldn't stay long, but he also couldn't resist a chance to talk with Emily.

He needed to alert her that the screen had been taken from behind the bushes, which meant someone had a pretty good idea what went on last night. Nothing was going according to plan this morning. He would have expected Emmett to be working with Calamity Sam by now, but something must have held up the program because the corral was still empty and Emmett was nowhere around.

Emily hurried up to him. "Did you find your hat?"

"No." The missing hat would be expensive to replace, but that wasn't even his biggest concern. Now that nobody had shown up with it, he hoped to hell it had been carried off by a raccoon.

He'd just seen Watkins, and he didn't have it, obviously. If some other cowboy had found it, then the guys could be planning to embarrass Clay. Cowboys loved to pull pranks, and unfortunately Clay could imagine someone announcing at the cookout that they'd found Clay's hat under Emily's window. Then things could get ugly.

"I'm sorry it's still missing," Emily said. "I wonder where it is."

"Yep, that's the big question."

"I have some other news. Watkins spent the night with Mary Lou."

"That's what the hands figured when he stayed out all night." Patches tossed his head and Clay tightened his hold on the lead rope.

"So you knew already?"

Clay lowered his voice. "Actually I missed the fact that he left the bunkhouse late in the evening and never made it back. The guys didn't miss it. This morning when his bunk hadn't been slept in, they all began to speculate whether he got lucky."

"I can see why you had to get back, then. They notice."

"Yep." Patches bumped Clay's shoulder with his nose. "Listen, Nick and I are about to do the collection, but it looks like you and Emmett haven't started with Calamity Sam yet."

"No. I gave him a birthday present and he wanted to take it back to his house."

"But everything's fine with him, right? He isn't acting strange or anything?"

"He's fine." She paused. "Well, when he first came into the kitchen, he had a funny look in his eye. Or maybe I was just imagining it. Are you worried he might know?"

"I'm worried that somebody knows. The bent screen is also gone."

"Oh!"

"Yeah, not good." Clay saw movement in the corral. "Emmett's back and he's turned out Sam, so you'd better get over there to help him."

"And you're doing the collection right now?"

"Yes. Nick's already in there."

"Let me ask my dad if he can spare me for a few minutes."

"You know, maybe you shouldn't. I know you want to watch this, but I have another collection scheduled for tomorrow morning. Let's see how everything looks then."

"You're worried, aren't you?"

He hated that he was responsible for the anxiety in her green eyes. And all the blame was his. He was the genius who'd decided to pay her a visit last night. He was the smart-ass who'd decided he needed to wear his best hat. And if he'd been more alert, he could have caught that screen instead of letting it bounce on the ground.

"I'm sorry, Emily. I hope I haven't put you in an impossible situation."

She smiled at him. "I'm not sorry. No matter what happens, it was worth it."

He let out a long breath. "Thanks for that. Now go help your dad."

"I will. Have fun with the AV, cowboy." With a wink, she turned and started off for the corral.

He watched her go way longer than he should have. If Patches hadn't jerked the lead rope, he might have watched even longer. If Emmett noticed him staring after Emily, Clay would be in deep trouble.

But she'd told him it was worth it. He'd hang on to that statement for dear life.

13

EMILY HALFWAY EXPECTED her dad to ask why she'd been talking to Clay, but he didn't. Instead he began instructing her on how they'd go about desensitizing Calamity Sam to the noise of a rustling plastic bag.

The yearling was a good-sized, gray-and-white paint, but he still looked gangly, like a teenager who needed to grow into his long legs. He had a gray patch over one eye that Emily found adorable. She would have liked to walk over and rub his silky-looking neck, but he was already eyeing the plastic bag warily, so she stayed back.

The routine was simple. Emily walked around the corral and shook the bag every so often. First she'd do it in front of the horse, then to one side, then the other, then in back. Meanwhile her dad held Sam's halter and talked soothingly to him. Whenever the colt was calm, Emmett gave him pieces of carrot as a reward.

They worked the program for fifteen-minute stretches, and then turned Sam loose to run around in the corral for a while and blow off steam. After that Emmett would snap the lead rope onto his halter and they'd repeat the process for another fifteen minutes.

By rights, Emily should have been bored. But she discovered that watching her father patiently coaxing Sam to accept the rattling plastic was fun. The horse was like a little kid, and she found herself laughing when he tried to get carrots he hadn't earned.

True, this was tame stuff compared to the noisy goings-on in the shed where Nick and Clay worked. Even though the shed stood quite a distance from the barn and the corral, the stallion's cries carried to where Emily and Emmett toiled with Sam. Emmett made no reference to it, acting as if he didn't hear the stallion.

After a while, the noise stopped. That probably meant Clay was using the AV on the stallion, and Emily really was curious as to how that all happened. Her curiosity would have to wait to be satisfied, though.

No doubt because she had sex on the brain lately, she worried about the stallion's satisfaction level. He'd been led to believe he could have the teaser mare, and she hoped the poor stud would get some fun out of the AV. She wondered if they warmed it somehow. If she got the opportunity, she'd ask Clay about that.

"Emily?"

"Yes?" She glanced at her father.

"You stopped rattling the bag."

"Sorry." Whoops. She'd have to be careful about staring off into space like that. She dutifully began rattling the plastic bag.

But as she moved around the corral, she caught sight of Clay walking out of the shed. Sure enough, he was

carrying the canister of semen on his shoulder as promised. He was like a walking advertisement for virility—
have semen, will travel.

"Emily?"

"Oh! Sorry, Dad!" She was seriously causing problems for herself. Her father might not have guessed that she was daydreaming about Clay earlier, but just now she'd been staring at the guy, so how much more obvious could she be?

She poured all her concentration into rattling that bag and somehow managed to ignore the tall cowboy walking across from the shed to the tractor barn on the other side of the corral. But still she knew, by keeping track from the corner of her eye, when he went inside.

"Break time," Emmett said. He unhooked the lead rope and Sam galloped around the corral, kicking up his heels.

On one circle he veered so close to Emily that she felt the wind of his passing. She rolled the plastic into a tight ball and jammed it down into her shorts pocket so that it was completely out of sight. Next time Sam came by, she called his name softly.

To her surprise, he wheeled and pranced toward her, his nostrils flared.

"Can I have a piece of carrot, Dad?" she asked. "I want to make a friend."

"Sure thing, Em." He walked over and gave her a couple of pieces.

Sam perked right up and ambled closer, sniffing loudly. Emily held one carrot back and put the other in her outstretched hand. The yearling's lips moved gently over her palm as he picked up the piece of carrot.

He turned his head to gaze at her while he crunched on it, and she could see herself reflected in his large brown eye. It was the eye with the gray patch, and it made him look like a war pony to her.

"Dad, I'm falling in love."

"What?" Concern echoed in that one-word question. "God, I hope not. You—"

"With Calamity Sam," she said before he could get any further into that response.

"Oh. That's different. But I'm afraid I can't buy him for you. He's worth a ton of money."

"I'm sure. He's beautiful." She didn't ask what her father had thought she'd meant. It was all too obvious, and she didn't want to discuss it.

"He's a good-looking colt, all right. Listen, sweetheart, since you have him eating out of your hand, I'm going to duck into the barn for a minute. Too much coffee this morning."

"Go ahead. I'll watch over this guy." After her dad left the corral, she gave Sam the other piece of carrot and finally got her wish of being able to stroke his soft neck. As she did, she talked softly to him and watched his ears flick back and forth as he listened to her, and then to other noises surrounding them.

"Looks like you've made a conquest."

She turned to discover Clay leaning against the rail. He'd stripped off his shirt again and looked like a fantasy cowboy with his snug jeans and his hat brim shading his dark eyes. Her heart thudded faster, both because he was so yummy and because he was tempting fate to even be here talking to her.

"You shouldn't stay," she said. "Dad will be back any minute."

"I'm sure he will. He doesn't walk off a job. But I saw you here alone and wanted to—"

"I know what you wanted. But it's dangerous to spend much time talking to each other, when *somebody* around here knows what's going on with us."

"You're right." He pushed away from the railing and his biceps flexed. "I'll leave."

"Did you get the semen?"

"Yeah."

"Is that AV heated?"

"A little. There's a surrounding cylinder for warm water. Why? Worried about the stallion's comfort?"

"It crossed my mind. I mean, how would you like somebody to shove your penis into a chilly artificial—"

"Emmett's coming back. See you later."

"Okay. And put on a shirt, will you? That's unfair."

"You're one to talk, standing there in shorts and a tight T-shirt."

"Bite me."

He kept his voice low. "If only I could. Later, sweet cheeks." Clay waved to Emmett. "Looks like Sam's coming along, Emmett."

"I think he is," Emmett called back.

Emily focused all her attention on Sam, rubbing his neck, scratching along the line of his mane, stroking his nose. "I think he likes me," she said as her father approached.

"I think he likes you a little bit too much, and I'm not talking about the horse."

"I know." She didn't look at him.

"I've said it before, but I'll say it again. The mistake your mother and I made was stupid, although I can't regret it because it gave us you. But to see you make the same mistake…"

"I won't, Dad."

"I wish I could be sure of that."

She took a deep breath and faced him. "I know you worry about Clay because he's an orphan and had such a difficult childhood, but he's not as fragile as you might think."

Emmett gazed at her, his expression troubled. "Of course I'm worried about him. I think the world of Clay, but he's not my kid. You are, and I don't want you tangled up in a messy situation."

And all this time she'd thought he might take sides against her because Clay was the son he'd never had, the cowhand he wished his daughter would be. Her chest tightened as she realized that he really did love her unconditionally. She didn't have to do anything special, or be anything special, to earn his love. She could make mistakes, and he'd still love her.

Gratitude flooded through her. "Thanks, Dad."

"Please be careful, sweetheart." He held her gaze for a moment longer, and then he turned to Sam. "And this squirt needs a lot more work. We'd better get to it."

Emily was happy to return to Sam's training. It was a

blissfully simple job. Meanwhile her life was becoming so complicated it made her head hurt.

CLAY HAD A REALLY BAD FEELING about how this day would end up, but he couldn't do a damned thing to prevent the disaster he sensed was coming. So he tried not to make it any worse and stayed as far away from Emily as possible for the rest of the morning. He even made a point of sitting at a different table during lunch.

But Emmett was called away after lunch to fix a plumbing problem for Pam over at the Bunk and Grub— another piece of the birthday plan falling into place. And Clay's determination to keep away from Emily was considerably weakened once her primary watchdog was no longer on the premises.

Because both Clay's hat and the screen had disappeared, he doubted that he'd be able to return to her room tonight. If he did, Emmett might be waiting with a shotgun. Maybe not literally, but the odds were good Clay would be shut out in some way.

Tomorrow Emmett would be on the ranch all day… and all night. The following day Emily would leave for Santa Barbara. The way Clay had it figured, he might have a window of opportunity this afternoon while Emmett was gone, and that would be it.

But he couldn't for the life of him figure out how to get her alone, even for twenty minutes. Now that Emmett was gone, the ranch had turned into Operation Central for getting this cookout show on the road.

Clay had been sent to the barn to organize saddles and make a list of who would ride which horse so mounting up would go like clockwork. Sarah didn't want to have any confusion that would give Emmett an excuse to try and call the whole thing off. Meanwhile Emily was up at the house working on the food angle and helping load boxes and coolers.

Fate seemed to be keeping them apart, and then, out of the blue, good fortune smiled on him. Emily appeared as he was counting saddles and making his list of guests and available horses.

"Sarah has decided that we need tiki torches to keep away the mosquitoes," she said. "We're running out of time, so she's commissioned you and me to drive quickly into town, pick up about ten from the feed store, and then go straight from there out to the picnic site and put them in the ground in a circle around the picnic area."

"Okay."

"She told me to make sure you didn't get picked up for speeding, though." Emily gazed at him. "Is that a problem with you?"

"Sometimes. A lookout would be a help." Clay calculated how fast he could drive and how much extra time he could buy them with this errand.

Emily held out a roll of bills. "I have the money, and we're supposed to leave right now."

"Give me five minutes."

"What, you need to finish your list?"

"No, I need to get something from the bunkhouse." He decided not to tell her what because she might protest that they didn't have time, but he'd make time. He could feel it running out, and he was a desperate man.

"Okay, I'll be in the truck. Hurry."

She didn't have to tell him that. In this case, every minute counted. Throwing down his pen, he left the barn and jogged the distance to the bunkhouse. He passed Watkins on the way.

"Could you finish up the list of which guest is riding which horse?"

"I can." Watkins smoothed his moustache. "Where are you off to in such a hurry?"

"Getting tiki torches to make a ring around the picnic site. For mosquitoes."

"I was wondering if anybody had thought of that. They could be bad out there."

"Sarah just did think of it." And he mentally thanked her for that, plus her decision to send Emily with him to watch for cops. She hadn't changed into jeans and boots yet, and that was all to the good.

In the bunkhouse, each ranch hand had a small dresser for his clothes and personal items. Clay pulled out a drawer and grabbed one condom. That's all he needed, all he had time for. He told himself to be grateful for this gift and not be greedy for more.

Somehow, in the next few hours, he had a hunch everything would come to light and he wasn't sure how he'd handle that with Emmett. But, as the old saying went, he might as well be hanged for a sheep as a lamb. Maybe he was wrong and he'd find himself able to climb that ladder to Emily's room tonight, after all.

But his instincts were good, honed from years of making sure he survived in any environment. Those instincts told him that the shit was about to hit the fan. Before it did, he wanted one last moment with Emily.

She was waiting in the truck when he hopped in and started the engine. "I think I know what you went for," she said.

"You probably do." He backed the truck around and headed for the dirt road.

"We don't have time for that. We'll do well to get the torches in the ground and return before Dad does."

He didn't say anything, and kept his speed down until he was about a half mile down the road, because he didn't want to send dust billowing around the ranch house. But when he was far enough away that it wouldn't be a problem, he hit the gas and sent up a rooster tail of dust.

"Clay! What in God's name are you doing?"

He glanced over at her and couldn't keep the grin off his face. "I'm hauling ass, sweet cheeks. Because we are going to use the condom in my pocket, or my name isn't Clay Whitaker."

She gripped the door handle and pushed down the lock. "You're going to end up in a ditch and break an axle, and then your name will be mud."

"No worries. When I first came to this ranch, there was a teenager living here by the name of Roni Kenway. She's a mechanic on the NASCAR circuit now, but while she was here, she loved souping up the ranch trucks and challenging any takers to a race. She taught a bunch of us how to drive fast."

"Good grief. I had no idea you were Dale Earnhardt Jr. in disguise."

"That's why Sarah sent me, but having me get a ticket

wouldn't help, so when we get on the main road, you'll need to keep your eyes peeled."

"Okay, but after we get those tiki torches, you're not going to be able to drive like a bat out of hell. You can't have them bouncing around and maybe breaking."

"Leave that to me. I'll tie them down. Cowboys are good with rope."

"I still don't see how we'll have time to fool around, Clay. We have to fill the torches and plant them in the ground, you know."

He had that figured out, too. "We'll have an assembly line. You fill and I'll ram them in the dirt. There's sort of a sexual rightness to that, don't you think?"

She shook her head. "I think you're fixated on sex, so anything would be sexual to you."

"You're probably right about that, but I have my reasons why I'm fixated."

"Yes, and they're all located below your belt."

He swerved around a curve, sending a plume of dust ten feet in the air. "That's also true." He took a deep breath. "Emily, there's no point in kidding ourselves. I'm afraid our happy little arrangement is going to be over very soon."

"That's a given. I'm leaving on Saturday."

"That's not what I mean. I'm talking about hours, not days."

"And what makes you say that?"

"It's just a feeling I have, that all hell is going to break loose. Your dad's going to find out about us. I don't know why I thought he wouldn't. Just cocky, I guess.

I'm not sure how the truth will come out, but I think it will. And once it does…"

"I hope you're wrong. I mean, it's his birthday."

"I know. And you want it to be all sweetness and light." Clay hit a straightaway and took it as fast as he dared, given that he was constantly on alert for critters crossing the road. Usually the loud roar of a racing engine sent them scurrying.

He raised his voice above the noise of the engine. "Did your dad say anything to you about me today?"

"Yes!" She had to yell to be heard. "He told me not to make the same stupid mistake he and my mother made!"

As the road began to curve, Clay slowed the truck again. "See, he knows. Whether he knows everything, I'm not sure. But somebody on the ranch has enough information to bring us down. It could happen any time."

"You're certainly a cheerful companion for this shopping trip."

"I'm just trying to make my case. I want to guarantee that I will hold you one more time. That's why I brought the condom."

"And where do you think you'll be able to accomplish this?"

"I don't know that yet. Not the picnic site. Even if no one's delivering stuff or arranging it, they would have left one of the hands to guard the place from critters. But I plan to make it happen. You can count on that. So, are you with me?"

"Yes, but—"

"That's all I need to know." Desire surged through him. "Now, hang on."

14

EMILY HUNG ON. WHEN THEY turned onto the asphalt road leading to Shoshone, she watched for any vehicle with lights mounted on the roof. Maybe because it was a Thursday instead of the weekend, they didn't see a single patrol car as Clay proceeded to demolish the speed limit.

Emily had always thought of the little town—located far enough from Jackson that it missed most of the tourist traffic—as boring because it didn't change much. Today she realized that having local families running the same businesses year after year gave the town a neighborly atmosphere.

She had no time to enjoy that, though, because Clay had the tiki torches tied down in the back of the truck before she'd finished paying for them.

"Ready?" he called from the doorway of the feed store.

She grabbed her change and thanked the man behind the counter.

"Welcome! I'll see you folks out there tonight!"

"Right!" Emily should have figured that most of the town was invited to the cookout. That's the way things worked around here. She dashed to the truck where Clay was holding the passenger door open for her. "I thought you'd be in the driver's seat ready to take off," she said as she hopped in.

"Just because I'm in a hurry doesn't mean I've forgotten my manners." He closed the door and jogged around the cab.

Emily smiled. *Cowboys. Gotta love 'em.* Then she blinked. Had that thought really gone through her mind? Yes, it certainly had, and she felt something give way inside her as years of dammed-up feelings began to surface.

She didn't hate cowboys, or the cowboy way of life. She didn't hate ranching or horses or dirt. That was her mother who disliked all those things. Emily had grown up hearing it, and somewhere along the way, she'd adopted her mother's prejudices as her own. Understandable, but still very sad.

"Are you watching for cops?"

She turned to him, joy washing through her as she recognized that she could love this man. She'd been battling the urge to do that because of who he was and where he lived. She didn't have to battle anymore. "No."

"Why not? And why are you grinning at me like that?"

"Because I just had an epiphany, which is amazing because I'm not standing on that sacred site you told me about."

"I'm happy for you, but if you don't help me look for the fuzz, we'll have a citation to go along with that epiphany."

"Okay. I can do that." But she couldn't wipe the smile off her face as she began scouring the side of the road for patrol cars lying in wait for the likes of Clay Whitaker.

"What's your epiphany?"

"I can't tell you yet." She wasn't about to blurt out that she was falling in love with him while he was barreling down the road and had to concentrate. "But I can tell you that I had a blast working with Calamity Sam this morning. I had no idea that my dad's job was that much fun."

"Just so you know, it's not all fun."

"So tell me all the down sides to working with horses." She probably needed a reality check to go along with her epiphany.

"Summers are great, but we still have to take care of the horses in the winter. We usually run ropes between the main buildings down to the barn, so if we get caught in a snowstorm, we won't get disoriented and freeze to death."

"Wow. Sounds like a challenge. Do you hate the winters, then?" She'd never been here during the winter. Maybe she'd hate that part.

"I don't, actually. The barn's heated, and working in there when the wind's howling outside is kind of cozy. In fact, being anywhere inside is cozy. We have a potbellied stove in the bunkhouse, and of course there's the big fireplace in the main house. Christmas is great.

The Chances always have a huge tree, and the hands put one up in the bunkhouse, too."

"So you're pretty much guaranteed a white Christmas every year."

"Yep." He was quiet for a moment. "Thinking of coming back for Christmas?"

"Yes. Yes, I am." She was thinking of doing far more than that, but it was a huge decision. She wanted to rush headlong into it, but she was trying to be more practical. "How do you feel about the riding part of your job?"

"Love it, especially when I have the chance to take a horse on a good run across the meadow. I feel like the king of the world when I can do that. Why?"

Excitement skittered down her spine. "I've never had the chance to ride like that. Dad was always worried about me falling, plus I refused to wear practical riding clothes and boots. But I'd like to try riding fast." Judging from the times she'd been on horseback, she could easily imagine substituting a galloping horse for a powerful wave. Everything was falling into place.

"Maybe tomorrow."

"That would be great." Riding with him would fit perfectly with her epiphany. "So what do you dislike about your work? Tell me all the bad stuff."

"Some people complain about shoveling manure, but I don't mind that. Others complain about getting up early, but I don't mind that, either. It's not a nine-to-five job, either. You never quite leave it."

"But if you're doing something you love, no matter what it is, you never quite leave it anyway, do you?"

He thought about that. "I suppose not."

"But I'm sure there's at least one really bad downside to your job."

"There is. Horses are more delicate than you'd think. They get sick. They die."

"Okay, that would be tough." She thought of Calamity Sam as he cavorted around the corral and tried to steal carrots. Yes, that would be a downside, for sure.

"It's hard both emotionally and financially," Clay said. "That's why I'm glad the Chances agreed to start collecting and shipping semen. When you depend entirely on the sale of horses, you're too vulnerable to illness and death. But semen is an asset that's not so likely to go south on you."

"Would you call it a liquid asset?" She was trying so hard not to laugh.

"Not always. Sometimes it's a frozen asset."

She couldn't tell from his tone whether he was kidding her or not, but she couldn't hold back her laughter another second. "Sorry," she managed through her giggles. "I know it's a serious subject, but—"

"No, it's not." He looked over at her and grinned. "Politics and religion are serious subjects. This is a conversation about horse ejaculate. How serious can that be?"

"I didn't want to mock what you do for a living."

"No mock taken. Still watching for cops?"

"I am, I promise, because you're still speeding."

"Yes, ma'am, I am." He hesitated. "Mind if I ask why all the questions about my job?"

"Just collecting data for my new project."

"Which is?"

"I'll tell you later. Oh, slow down, slow down! There's a patrol car off to the right side of the road."

"I see it." He let up on the gas.

Emily held her breath as they drove past the cop. When the patrol car stayed on the side of the road and didn't pull out after them, she sighed in relief. "I *really* don't want us to get a ticket."

"Us?"

"Well, you would get the ticket, of course, but—"

"It's okay. You don't have to explain. I liked that you said *us*."

"Me, too."

CLAY DIDN'T KNOW WHAT TO THINK. All this talk about an epiphany followed by a bunch of questions about raising horses for a living told him that something was going on in that beautiful head of hers. She might be thinking that life on a ranch wasn't so bad, after all.

He could thank himself for that, because good sex could have a powerful effect on a person. From what he'd gathered from Emmett, good sex had been part of why Emmett and Jeri had decided to get married, even though Jeri wasn't the ranching type. Emmett had been so worried about history repeating itself, and now it seemed like a legitimate concern.

Clay had never consciously set out to change Emily's mind about ranch life, but motivations were tricky things. Deep down, he might have hoped that she'd start thinking more kindly about cowboys in general and him in particular. He might have gotten his wish, and now he had to deal with the potential problem he'd caused for both of them.

He couldn't pretend anymore that this was all about sex. He was falling for her. Her use of the word *us* had demonstrated how fast he was falling, because he'd loved hearing her say it. He wanted to hear her say it some more.

But whatever this supposed epiphany was, she couldn't trust it. Her hormones were in control, not her brain, and at some point he'd have to tell her that. Depressing as that thought was, it was followed by one even more depressing. All things considered, he shouldn't have sex with her again.

He shouldn't have surrendered to temptation in the first place, but that was water under the bridge. No sense in beating himself up for something that he couldn't change. He could change his current plan, though, so he wouldn't add fuel to the fire.

"You're quiet all of a sudden," she said.

"Just thinking."

"Anything I need to know about?"

"Not yet."

"That's enigmatic."

"Oh, you know cowboys. We're the strong, silent type." He turned right onto the dirt road leading to the ranch. The entrance, with its poles on either side of the road and another over the top to hold the Last Chance Ranch sign, always gave his heart a lift as he drove through it.

He hoped maybe Emily could feel the same someday. But she had to love the ranch for itself, and not because she'd fallen for him and wanted to find a way they could be together.

"Hold on," he said. "I'm going to speed up."

"Go for it." Her green eyes sparkled under the shade of her straw hat.

If only he could. He gripped the wheel and stepped on the gas. He concentrated on his driving and tried not to think about Emily sitting there beside him.

He'd promised her they'd have sex, but it was a promise he'd have to break, for her sake and maybe for his, too. After bragging about how easily he could protect himself emotionally, he'd done a piss-poor job of it. He'd known she'd be sexy, but he hadn't counted on her being fun and endearing. Bottom line, he was already dreading the day she drove away.

The trip to the picnic site was a wild ride, but not for the reason he'd originally given Emily. He wanted to be finished with this job so he could take her back to the house and put some distance between them. Nobility would be far easier when she wasn't close enough to touch.

But he wouldn't leave her hanging, either. She shouldn't have to wonder why he'd changed his mind. He didn't play those kinds of games. So instead of making love to her, he'd explain exactly why he wasn't doing that.

"Wow, it looks different out here," she said as they pulled up behind one of the ranch trucks.

"It better look different. The party's in a few hours." He got out and waved at Jeb, a young ranch hand with red hair and freckles. Jeb must have been assigned to guard duty because he was sitting on a bench talking on his cell phone.

By the time he came around the truck to let Emily out, she'd opened the door and was ready to hop down. "Your manners are wonderful." She jumped to the grassy edge of the road. "But we need to get this done."

"Hey, I can help." Jeb walked toward the truck, tucking his cell phone in his jeans pocket as he approached. "Sarah just called and said you'd be coming with tiki torches. In fact, I can take care of the whole job if you want. There's nothing much else to do out here and I'm supposed to stay until everyone rides out."

Clay took a look around. Wood was piled in both fire pits, and every table was decorated with a red checkered oilcloth attached to it with metal clamps. One table held boxes of nonperishables, and the coolers were stacked in the back of the ranch truck with a tarp over them.

Jeb shrugged. "It's all done. I may drag some fallen tree branches out here from the woods and chop them up for extra firewood, but other than that, we're good to go." He glanced at Emily. "It's sure nice that you could make it for your dad's birthday, Emily."

She smiled at him. "I'm glad I could, too. It's Jeb, right?"

"Yes, ma'am." His face was shaded by his hat, but that didn't completely disguise the blush that made his freckles disappear. "Saw you working with Calamity Sam this morning."

"I had fun."

"Yes, ma'am. That yearling is lots of fun. I remember one time he managed to let himself out of the corral. I had to chase him all over the yard, but I finally caught him. And then there was this other time when he—"

"Sorry to interrupt, but we'd better get going." Clay knew that if he didn't say something, Jeb would keep talking forever, just to maintain a connection with Emily. Clay had been like Jeb ten years ago—totally infatuated. "So if you'll help unload the torches and set them up for us, that would be great. Sarah wants them in a circle surrounding the picnic tables."

"I know." Jeb nodded. "For the mosquitoes. That's a really good idea. Emily, I don't know if you've experienced Wyoming mosquitoes, but they—"

"With luck we won't experience them tonight," Clay said. "Let's get those torches unloaded so you can start putting them up."

"You bet." Jeb seemed to take the hint and headed for the back of the truck. When Emily followed him, he paused. "You don't need to be hauling torches, Emily. Clay and I can handle this."

Emily exchanged an amused glance with Clay. "Thanks, Jeb. I'll go relax in the truck."

"You do that." Jeb proceeded to unload the torches with as much swagger as possible, carrying one on each shoulder over to the picnic tables.

Clay sighed, understanding the impulse far too well. He wasn't so different from Jeb, after all. This morning he'd paraded across Emily's line of vision carrying the collection canister on his shoulder because she'd commented on how manly he'd looked doing it the day before.

Once the torches were unloaded, Clay shook hands with Jeb and climbed back in the truck. "That's done."

"Yes." She gave him a sideways glance filled with meaning. "That's done. Now what?"

He started the truck and made a U-turn so they were headed back toward the ranch house. "Now we find a private place to talk."

She laughed. "Talk? That isn't the way you presented it before."

"I know. But we do need to talk."

"Actually, I agree. But we have extra time now that Jeb's setting up the torches. We should have time to talk, and…do other things."

He stifled a groan.

"Unless you don't want to do those other things anymore?"

"I do. You have no idea how much. It's just…let's wait until I can pull off the road. I want to be far enough away that Jeb doesn't realize what we're doing."

"I'm for that."

The meadows were crisscrossed with various temporary roads that were nothing more than two indistinct tire tracks. Clay found one off to the right and took it. As he recalled, this one curved around behind a line of pine trees, so the truck would be out of sight.

The road turned as he'd remembered, and he drove until he was satisfied with the level of privacy. Then he switched off the engine and unfastened his seat belt. "Let's get out and walk a bit." He laid his hat on the dash.

"Walk? I thought cowboys hated to walk."

"Humor me."

"Sure." She unfastened her seat belt and followed his example, putting her hat on her side of the dashboard.

"And let me help you out."

"I can do that, too."

He thought about what to say and how to say it as he rounded the truck and opened her door. But once she placed her hand in his and he helped her down, all thoughts went out of his head, and he pulled her close with a groan, cradling her head against his chest while he fought the need to kiss her.

She wrapped her arms around him. "What's wrong, Clay? Is it that you're worried about my dad? Because I would never let him take this out on you. And, anyway, I don't think we have to worry about that."

"It's not your dad."

She lifted her head and gazed up at him. "Then what is it? You seem very upset."

He looked into those glorious green eyes. "It's you I'm worried about, Emily. I think I know what your epiphany is all about, and I'm afraid you're not thinking very clearly right now."

Her lips firmed. "Since you seem to be able to read my mind, would you care to tell me what's muddled about my thinking?"

"I don't mean to insult you. I'm just trying to help."

"Help me think?"

"Help you realize that our lovemaking has cast a rosy glow over your whole ranch experience, making you see things through that filter. That's no way to make a decision that could affect the rest of your life."

"What decision?"

"About moving here. About being with me."

She stiffened in his arms. "Forgive me for assuming you might welcome that idea."

"God, I'm saying this all wrong. I would love to have you here. You have to know that."

She backed out of his arms. "I'm having a little trouble believing it while you're harping on the rosy glow that's skewed my thinking all to hell and gone."

"But isn't that what happened to your mother?"

She stared at him. "My mother had never been to Wyoming in her life. She came out on vacation, met my dad, and on the basis of great sex she decided to marry him and live here."

"Exactly."

"Clay, that is *nothing* like my situation. I've been coming to this ranch ever since I was old enough to travel by myself on a plane. My dad is a cowboy."

"But—"

"Let me finish. I have ranching in my blood, whether I wanted to acknowledge that before or not. My mother has been telling me for years that I don't want this life, and her brainwashing has worked until now, when I've finally begun to think for myself. You—" she paused to point a finger at him "—are the icing on the cake, but you're not the cake! This ranch and my ties to it are the cake. Got that?"

"Yeah, but if we hadn't made love, I wonder if you would feel the same."

She threw her hands in the air. "Maybe not! Maybe I like icing on my cake! So is that why you're reconsidering having sex with me right now? You're worried there's too much icing?"

He rubbed the back of his neck, more confused than ever. "I don't know. Maybe."

"Well, heaven forbid that could happen. Take me back to the ranch house. I have a party to get ready for."

He reached for her. "Emily, I didn't mean to imply that you aren't capable of making a good decision. I just—"

"Oh, you didn't imply anything." She backed out of reach. "You flat-out said it. And because I don't relish having sex with someone who thinks my brain's so addled with hormones that I can't think straight, I'm glad you decided against using that condom. Let's go." She turned and climbed back into the truck and closed the door with a loud bang.

Uncertain what to say or do, he had no choice but to walk back around to the driver's side, get in and start the engine. He hadn't expected this conversation to be a lot of fun, but he'd hoped they'd be able to discuss things rationally.

He put on his hat, and she grabbed hers and crammed it down over her shiny hair.

"Emily, I just think you need to take more time before you come to any conclusions. That's all I'm saying."

She stared out the windshield. "Just drive, Whitaker. And make it fast. I know you're good at that."

Cursing under his breath, he backed the truck around and headed toward the ranch road. Once on it, he drove as fast as he dared. He could hardly wait for this ride to end. Being noble truly sucked.

15

EMILY CHOSE NOT TO SAY anything more on the ride back to the ranch, and she hopped out of the truck before Clay had shut off the motor. She left with a curt goodbye and thank you. Clay had tarnished her shiny new epiphany, and she was furious with him for doing that.

She wondered how she ever could have thought she was falling in love with a guy who had such a low opinion of her reasoning ability. The argument had clarified her thinking nicely, though. She'd discovered an affinity for horses and for ranch life in general.

For the first time in her life she felt excited about a career option, and she had a built-in mentor. She would ask her dad if she could move here and apprentice herself to him. She figured he'd be thrilled.

Because of all the money she'd saved, she wouldn't need a salary for quite a while. Her living quarters might be an issue, but maybe she could rent one of the vacant rooms in the main house from Sarah. As for

Clay, she'd learn to enjoy her cake without icing, thank you very much.

Fortunately nobody was in the living room when she walked into the house, because she was in no mood to talk to anyone. Mary Lou had run Emily's jeans through the washer and dryer this morning while she was working with Calamity Sam, so she'd take a hot shower and get dressed for the party. She wouldn't mention her idea to her father until tomorrow, when they could find some quiet time to sit down and make plans.

Maybe she wouldn't have to confront him about the fake inheritance, after all. She could simply say she'd saved a lot of money over the years, which would fund her apprenticeship. And once she was working here, he wouldn't need to send her any more. That way she could save his pride.

Being on the premises would make it easier for her to encourage his romance with Pam, too. But Emily didn't intend to mention Pam to her mother. Jeri would be unhappy enough about the move without the added news about her ex's new girlfriend.

Emily could soften the blow of leaving Santa Barbara with frequent trips back there, but she'd spent the first twenty-seven years of her life within a short distance of her mom's front door. She'd thought her mother needed her, and perhaps she did, but so did her father. And Emily's future was here at the Last Chance.

Climbing the curved staircase, she walked down the hallway to her bedroom. Before she reached it, she knew someone was in there fiddling with her window. She recognized the sounds after all the action that window'd had the night before. No doubt the person in her room was replacing the screen.

She knew for a fact it wasn't Clay. She paused, not sure if she wanted to find out who it was. She could always go back downstairs and…and what? Lurk around watching to see who came down the staircase?

No, that was cowardly. If she hoped to work at the Last Chance, she might as well own up to damaging the screen and get that behind her. She'd rather not admit exactly *how* it was damaged, but maybe she wouldn't have to.

Then again, maybe she'd have to confess all… When she walked into the room, she found her father fastening a new screen into place. His hat was lying on the bed. Next to it was a brown Stetson.

She cleared her throat, in case he hadn't heard her footsteps. "Hi, Dad."

"Hello, Emily." He finished adjusting the screen and turned around.

"Thanks for doing that." How lame that sounded, but she wasn't sure where to start.

"It needed doing. I had to go help Pam with a plumbing issue, so while I was buying an elbow joint for her bathroom sink, I picked up a new screen for the window."

"You're probably disappointed in me."

"Actually I'm more disappointed in myself. If I'd been more involved in your life, you might be more inclined to listen to my advice. As it stands, I can't really blame you for ignoring me. Why should you pay attention to a guy who's spent maybe thirty days with you all told since you were a toddler?"

"Dad, I've just figured something out. If you have a minute, I'd like to tell you about it."

"I have as long as it takes."

Her throat tightened with love for this man. He'd loved her so much from afar, and he hadn't been willing to make her the battleground between him and Jeri. He'd simply abandoned the field.

"I need to start by saying that what I'm about to ask has nothing whatsoever to do with Clay."

"Okay."

From the way he said it, she knew he didn't believe that. But she plowed ahead anyway, explaining how she felt about the ranch and why she wanted to become his apprentice. "And I have a fair amount of money saved, so I wouldn't need a salary for at least the first year."

His eyes widened. "A year? Really?"

"I haven't spent all you gave me. I've been investing." She decided to substitute *all* for *any* and hope he wouldn't question that.

Fortunately he didn't. "You must be one hell of an investor."

"I am, actually. But I don't want to go into that field, if that's what you might be thinking. It's fun to do it for myself, and I'd be happy to help you if you want, but I know now that I need an outdoor job. I basically want to do what you're doing."

"You might need to get in line. At one time Jack said he wanted my job when I'm done with it. That might have changed now that he's settled in with Josie, but that's what he said once."

Emily shrugged. "Then I'll be one of the hands for as long as they'll have me. I really don't care. But I've discovered I love it here. I love not having to dress in business clothes and sit behind a desk. I love that I could walk out my front door and be at work."

"The weather's not always so balmy, you know."

"That's what Clay said." Instantly she regretted bringing Clay's name back into the conversation.

"So he knows about your plan?"

"Not really. He got an inkling of what I had in mind and told me I didn't know what I was talking about."

Emmett sighed. "I'm afraid he's right. Look, I know you're involved with him, and you think that you can just change your life around to accommodate that, but—"

"No, Dad! That's why I said right away that he has nothing to do with this. As far as I'm concerned, Clay and I are finished."

"Finished? You barely got started!"

"We shouldn't have started at all. Now he's convinced that the only reason I want to move here is because of him. How's that for an ego?"

Emmett folded his arms. "Can you honestly tell me that you would have come to this conclusion if Clay hadn't been part of the picture?"

"Obviously I can't. He's been part of my experience, so of course that had to have some bearing. But he's not *the* reason I want to move here. This is not a replay of you and Mom. I wouldn't care if he moved to…I don't know…Texas."

"Emily, he won't do that, and you know it. This is the place that became his first home, and that's why he came back after he finished school. You couldn't pry him away from this ranch with a crowbar. So if you move to the Last Chance, you'll be running into Clay all the time. And I think that's what you have in mind."

Now it was her turn to cross her arms. "No, it isn't."

Sarah's voice drifted up the stairs. "Emily, are you up there? I talked to Clay, and he said you two delivered the tiki torches."

"We did!" Emily glanced at her dad and lowered her voice. "Does she know you're up here replacing the screen."

"No. I made sure the coast was clear."

"Well, I'm here, now, so we can make it look like you came to see me." She walked out into the hall and over to the top of the stairs to peer down at Sarah. "My dad and I were up here having a father-daughter chat, but if you need me for something, let me know."

Sarah beamed at her. "Good girl," she said softly. "Keep him occupied for a little longer. We're lining the horses up on the far side of the house so he won't see them until the last minute." Sarah made a circle of her thumb and forefinger, winked at Emily, and walked out the front door.

Emily walked back into the bedroom. She might not get that hot shower, after all.

"Something's cooking, isn't it?" Emmett gazed at her.

"What makes you think that?"

"The way everyone's concerned with keeping me busy all of a sudden."

"Well, I'm not. I just want to know if you'll hire me, at no pay, as your apprentice."

"Emily, I think you're making a big—"

"What have you got to lose? You'll get to see a lot of me, you'll get some free help around here—even if I'm not very good at first—and if I find out after a few months that I don't like it, you're out nothing and I've spent a little money and time finding out it doesn't work for me."

"But you will have quit your job and, I assume, given up your apartment."

"So what? I don't much like the job or the apartment. I can easily find another one of each if I really can't stand it here."

"Let me think about it. I need to get out of here while Sarah's otherwise occupied." He started toward the door.

"Wait."

"For what?"

"You forgot your hat." She picked it up and held it out. "And what about the other one?"

"I thought you should give it to him. Less awkward that way."

She held out both hands, palms up. "No, thanks."

"Oh, for crying out loud, Emily. You could give him back the hat."

"I won't be rude to him in public, but I really can't see myself returning his hat. I'd appreciate it if you would."

"He's not going to like getting this hat from me."

"He won't be as surprised as you think. He knows somebody found it, and that somebody also made off with the damaged screen. He's worried that it'll all come out publicly at the party tonight."

"Good God!" Emmett stared at her in shock. "I would never embarrass you two like that!"

She dredged up a smile. "Thanks for that. But I really think you need to return the hat and talk to him. That way, you'll find out I'm right. Hope for a relationship with Clay is not my motivation for coming to the Last Chance. I'm sure he knows that now." She picked up Clay's hat and extended it toward her father.

"Maybe you're right." He took the hat and tucked it under his arm. "I suppose while I'm at it I should also ask him his intentions toward my daughter. That's what dads are supposed to do."

"Well, I'm not sure you want to ask him *that*." She didn't think Emmett wanted to know what Clay's intentions were, or what they had been, before he'd decided sex was rotting her brain.

"I'll talk with him," he said. "I'll find out his stand on all this." He paused. "Do you want me to give him any message?"

"No." That sounded too abrupt. "No, thank you."

"Okay, then. Guess I'll be riding with someone else instead of driving myself to the Spirits and Spurs, so let's try to get in the same vehicle."

"You bet." She was astounded that her dad, who had been alert enough to discover that Clay had climbed through her bedroom window last night, hadn't figured out that the Spirits and Spurs plan was a decoy. Maybe that was her doing, hers and Clay's. Emmett was so worried about his daughter and Clay making a mess of their lives that he'd missed the cues that his birthday would be in a whole other venue. She walked over and gave him a quick hug. "See you soon, Dad."

Maybe it was mean of her to send him off with that hat, but he and Clay had their own relationship to work out. They needed to come to terms with what had happened and get beyond it. That was her goal, and it should be theirs, too.

CLAY SAT IN THE DRIVEWAY for a while after Emily made her chilly exit and wondered if he could have done anything better. Maybe not. He still thought she was making a snap decision based partly, if not completely, on what they'd shared.

He might be a fool for not embracing her cockeyed plan. If he'd been enthusiastic instead of discouraging, things would be a whole lot more pleasant—at least for the short term.

But the fun wouldn't have lasted long. Emmett was bound to be suspicious of her sudden change of heart, especially given her poorly disguised interest in Clay. Plain and simple, Clay felt responsible for Emily's supposed epiphany. He'd owed Emmett the courtesy of trying to talk her out of it.

Thinking about Emmett reminded him that the foreman's birthday party would start soon. Clay wasn't in the mood for a party, but he could fake it. He should also check how Watkins had made out with the lists.

After parking the truck, Clay went looking for Watkins in the horse barn. He found the place virtually deserted. Apparently the horses had already been saddled and taken to the agreed-upon gathering spot at the far end of the house, a place Emmett wasn't likely to look.

Scanning the yard for any sign of Emmett, Clay walked quickly from the barn to the house and hurried around to the east side. Sure enough, a string of saddled horses was there, with a couple of the guys keeping track of them until the appointed hour.

Since everything seemed to be under control, Clay gave them a wave and started back toward the bunkhouse. But skidded to a stop when he saw Emmett coming down the steps of the ranch house. The foreman was carrying Clay's brown Stetson. Shit.

He decided to stay where he was and see what Emmett did. Emmett was headed in the direction of the bunkhouse. If he walked in and didn't come back out right away, Clay would follow. Although, with the party coming up so soon this didn't seem like the best time to discuss Clay's relationship with Emily.

Emmett disappeared into the bunkhouse with the hat. He came out seconds later without it. Clay sighed in relief. They'd have to talk about Emily sometime, but not right now.

Clay had known in his gut that Emmett had found the hat, and likely the screen, too. He wondered if the foreman had already talked to Emily. She'd probably run into him on the way to her room.

Clay wanted to know how that conversation had

gone, but he'd have to wait to find out. He needed a quick shower and a change of clothes. At least he could wear his best hat to the party.

16

BY THE LIGHT OF A ROARING bonfire, Emily watched her dad open his presents. He took his own sweet time with each one and tolerated the heckling with a good-natured smile. For a guy who tended to avoid being the center of attention, he seemed to be thoroughly enjoying himself.

One of the hands had bought him the expected whoopee cushion, and he'd been sitting on it ever since. Every time he shifted his weight, the cushion bleated, causing a roar of laugher from the hands. It was silly and fun, exactly as a sixtieth should be.

Sarah approached, a wine bottle in one hand and her own plastic goblet in the other. The guys mostly had beer, but Sarah had provided wine for those who preferred it. "Need me to top that off, Emily?"

"Thanks, but I'm fine. Listen, I can take that bottle and go around checking on the wine drinkers. You should relax after all the work you've done."

"It's okay. I love being the hostess. But thanks for offering. It's gone well, don't you think?"

"Beautifully. I can't believe how surprised he was when you took him around the house and he saw the horses all saddled and ready to go." Emily held up her pocket-size camera. "I know Dominique's the official photographer, but I wanted some, too. I got that one, for sure."

"Good. It never hurts to have more than one camera in the mix."

"That's why I brought mine," Pam said, coming over to stand beside Sarah. "I'm following you, wine lady. I need a refill."

"My pleasure." Sarah poured wine into Pam's glass. "I was just telling Emily that I think this turned out great."

"It sure did. It took more advance planning than the Normandy Invasion, but the results are outstanding." She glanced over at Emily. "Having you here is the crowning touch. I don't want to lay a guilt trip on you, but I know he'd love to have you visit more often."

"Funny you should mention that." During the party Emily had realized that the person with the power around here was Sarah Chance. If Sarah agreed that Emily could become an unpaid employee, then everyone else would have to fall in line. Emily had been talking to the wrong people.

"Oh, good," Pam said. "Are you saying you'll be here next summer? Or how about Christmas? It's beautiful here during the holidays."

"Actually," she turned to the woman who could give them both the answer they wanted to hear. "I was wondering if I could rent a room from you, Sarah, and start learning the horse business."

Sarah didn't look as surprised as Emily might have thought she would. Instead she exchanged a glance with Pam. "See? I told you she'd started to like it here."

"I love it here. I probably always have, but I've been hearing all my life that ranching was wrong for me and I wouldn't let myself see the truth." She paused for a breath. "And before we get any further in the discussion, this isn't about Clay."

Sarah gave her an understanding smile. "Not even a little bit?"

"All right, it was a little bit at first, but he said I don't know my own mind, so he's not my favorite person right now."

Pam chuckled. "No woman likes a man telling her she's not thinking straight. I'm still trying to teach Emmett that lesson."

"I dearly hope you succeed, Pam." Emily turned back to Sarah. "I have money for rent and food, so I wouldn't need a salary for at least a year, maybe longer. I've saved…most of what my dad's been sending me, and I've invested it. So I'd be free help for as long as it takes me to learn the job."

Sarah gave her a long look. "You realize a lot of people on the ranch think you've been soaking your dad for years and squandering his hard-earned cash."

"Clay told me. But I'm not that kind of person."

"I've known that from the moment I found out you drove seventeen hours to get here so you wouldn't have to spend money on a motel." Sarah grinned. "That's your dad all over."

"This afternoon at my house," Pam said, "he couldn't say enough about the way you worked with Calamity Sam. But he's worried about you and Clay. He thinks you'll make the same mistake your mother made. You'll hook up with a cowboy and then find out this life isn't for you."

"But I don't see that happening," Sarah said. "Do you, Pam?"

"No, I don't. I saw you helping Mary Lou grill those steaks tonight. Then you ran around making sure everybody had bread and coleslaw. I've watched your face tonight, Emily. You're in your element, aren't you?"

"Exactly!" Joy bubbled in her at finding someone who understood. "I've never been able to figure out my place in this world because I refused to consider that the ranch was it. But it is…if Sarah will have me."

"I would be delighted. When do you want to start?"

"Is tomorrow okay?"

Sarah laughed. "I thought you'd want to go home and take care of things there first."

"But this is home."

"That's nice to hear, but I only meant—"

"I know, and I'll make some calls tomorrow. The most important one will be to my mother."

Sarah took a swallow of wine. "She won't like this."

"No, but I'll visit. Once she understands how happy

I am here, she'll be okay with it. I hope so, anyway."
Emily couldn't let herself be sidetracked by what her
mother wanted. She'd done that all her life.

"Well, I think this deserves a toast." Pam raised her
glass. "Here's to going after what you want."

"I'll drink to that." Sarah touched her glass to Pam's
and winked.

"Me, too." Emily clicked her glass against each of
theirs. "Thank you. Thank you both for all the support.
And by the way, Pam, I intend to help you get what you
want, too."

Pam held her gaze. "Thank you. He's a stubborn
one."

"Who thinks you don't know your own mind," Emily
added.

"Yes. But if you and I put our minds together…"

Emily smiled. "He'll be a goner."

"This is going to be fun to watch," Sarah said. "And
speaking of watching, Clay hasn't taken his eyes off you
all night, Emily."

"Maybe he's waiting for me to do something stupid."

Sarah glanced in Clay's direction. "So do something
smart. Go over there and tell him you're staying, whether
he thinks it's a good idea or not. Let him know you don't
need his approval."

Pam grinned. "Sarah Chance, you are a troublemaker."

"But she's right," Emily said. "Instead of getting
angry when he said my plan was bad, I should have
laughed and said I was doing it anyway." She drained
her wineglass and tossed it in a nearby trash barrel. "But

it's not too late. I can still say that. Excuse me, ladies. I have a man to put in his place."

CLAY HAD TRIED TO IGNORE Emily. He'd really tried. Turned out it was humanly impossible. He loved watching her move through the crowd, her borrowed straw cowboy hat at a jaunty angle, her smile charming everyone she met.

He'd noticed each time she laughed, and how the reflection of the firelight in her long blond hair. She'd seemed thrilled when Watkins had tuned up his guitar, and she'd participated with gusto in the sing-alongs. Many of the tunes were old cowboy songs, and she didn't know all the words, but she'd chimed in happily when the chorus arrived.

If he'd expected her to retreat into a shell because he'd shot down her plan, she didn't seem willing to oblige. He'd noticed Emmett watching her, too, a fond expression in his eyes. Emmett hadn't looked quite so happy when he'd glanced at Clay, though. The foreman was worried, and Clay regretted that.

Emmett had thanked him after unwrapping the leather gloves, but other than that, he hadn't said much. Clay didn't blame him. He'd complicated Emmett's life, and at some point he needed to ask for forgiveness. But bringing up problems wasn't what tonight was about.

That's why he couldn't figure out what Emily had in mind when she tossed away her wineglass and started in his direction. Surely she wasn't coming over to apologize for her angry response this afternoon. Was it possible she'd decided he was right and wanted to tell him so?

Funny, but that thought didn't make him feel very good. If he'd been right in his assessment, then she'd leave and might not be back for quite a while. Years, even… Suddenly he didn't want to be right. He wanted to be dead wrong.

She walked up to him and tilted her hat back so she could look him straight in the eye. "I'm staying," she said.

"Staying?" He wasn't sure what she meant. "You mean through the weekend?"

"No, I mean for good. I've talked to Sarah and she's fine with it. I'll rent the room I'm in and start learning how to train cutting horses. I start tomorrow."

His heart raced out of control. This was exciting, but so full of pitfalls, too. "Does Emmett know about this?"

"He knows that's what I want to do, but not that I've made a decision to do it and confirmed it with Sarah."

Clay hesitated. There were minefields all around him. "Uh, shouldn't you have checked with him first?"

"You know what? No. I asked him about it this afternoon, basically giving him the right to say whether I could or not, and he said he'd think about it."

"Sounds reasonable."

"It's a delaying tactic, and I'm tired of having my life on hold. Now that I know what I want, I'm impatient to get going. Tonight I realized that the person who ultimately gets to decide is not my dad, but Sarah. She's the boss lady, and it's her house I'd like to rent space in. So I asked her."

"That takes *cojones*, Emily."

"I'll tell you what it takes." She shoved her hands in the back pockets of her jeans and squared her shoulders. "It takes a woman who knows her own mind. And I do, Clay Whitaker. I most certainly do."

"I love you." The words spilled out before he knew they were coming.

Her eyes widened. "Did you just say what I think you said?"

"Yeah." He let out a breath and his whole body relaxed. There it was, out in the open. Just as well have it that way. "I love you. That may seem quick, but it's not. I've been half in love with you since I was eighteen, but then I really got to know you, and…I'm crazy about you, Emily."

A slow smile tilted the corners of her mouth. "And you couldn't have told me that this afternoon?"

"Are you kidding? That would have been the worst thing I could have done. Talk about stacking the deck! But now that you've planted yourself on this ranch, whether I like it or not, I'm free to say…I like it, Emily."

She glanced over her shoulder at the rowdy group gathering around Watkins as he tuned up his guitar. "They're starting another sing-along."

"You seemed to really enjoy that."

She turned back to him. "I did, but I think I'll skip this one. What do you say we step into the shadows for a few minutes?"

He knew he was grinning like a fool and couldn't help it. "You are getting assertive, Miss Sterling."

"I've discovered that's the only way for a girl to get

what she wants." She gave him a little shove on the chest.

He stepped back out of the light given off by the bonfire and the tiki torches. "And what is it you want, Emily?"

"You, cowboy." And she grabbed him around the neck and put him in a lip-lock.

Judging from the way she was kissing him, he thought he was going to love this new, more aggressive Emily even more than he had the California surfer girl who hadn't known quite who she was or where she belonged. But he needed to get a few things straight, so he reluctantly lifted his mouth from hers.

She tried to pull his head down again.

"Wait. I want to ask you something. Is this all about sex?"

"It's partly about sex."

"I need more than that, Emily."

She chuckled. "Isn't that supposed to be my line?"

"Yes, and for some reason you're not saying it. I've laid my heart at your feet. So far yours is still safely tucked away. That won't work."

She cupped his face in both hands and her voice gentled. "I was going to tell you this afternoon, but then you insulted my intelligence."

"I'm sorry. I didn't give you credit for—"

"For being smart enough to know what's good for me?"

"Basically."

"That's right, you didn't. But before you made those

patronizing remarks, I'd planned to tell you that a significant part of my epiphany…was you."

He couldn't believe how his soul thirsted for the words, the three little words that would make all the difference. "And what about me?"

"I haven't been dreaming about you for ten years, so I can't say that, but I have been hearing about you from my dad for a long time. Sure I was jealous, but I admired you and all you'd accomplished. And then I discovered you are awesome in bed, and you have a great sense of humor, and you carry a canister of horse semen better than anyone I know."

"Okay, so my résumé looks pretty good." *Say it, Emily!* "Anything to add to that?"

"Only that I love you desperately and can hardly wait to see how everything turns out between us now that I'll be staying here right under your nose. Is that what you were angling for?"

"Uh-huh." He tightened his arms around her and thanked his lucky stars for Emily. "But instead of being under my nose, I'd rather have you just under me, period. Do you think we could arrange that?"

"I have to find out from Sarah if I'm allowed to entertain men in my room. I can't have you climbing up and down that rope ladder anymore. It's hard on the screens."

He gazed down at her. "So I'm not dreaming this? You're really staying?"

"Yes."

"Then don't just ask if you can entertain a man in

your room, like I'll be a guest." His mouth hovered over hers.

"Why not?"

"Because I want my own key." And then he kissed her as the birthday party crowd sang "Home on the Range." He'd thought that the Last Chance was his home, but now he knew where his home truly was—here in Emily's arms.

Epilogue

The following week

EMILY HELD THE LEAD ROPE as a black-and-white stallion named Rorschach mounted the dummy. Clay moved in with the collection canister with its warm AV, and Rorschach filled it. Emily still planned to learn how to train cutting horses, but because she'd been so fascinated with the semen collection process, Clay had suggested she might want to be his assistant now and then.

That worked for her. It seemed as if the mornings she helped him fill that canister affected them that night, making them more crazy for each other than usual. She'd decided not to point that out because this was supposed to be a clinical operation with no sexual overtones. But she knew better, and she thought Clay did, too.

Rorschach finished up and they let him rest on the dummy. Clay had set up a couple of sawhorses nearby where he could set the canister temporarily so he didn't have to hold it while they waited for Rorschach to recover. Emily wasn't quite ready to have

Clay leave her alone to deal with a valuable stallion and a teaser mare.

"My mom's sending a box of my clothes over," she said. "I don't know how much of it I can wear around here, but it'll be good to get some of my underwear, at least."

Clay wiggled his eyebrows. "I love it when you talk dirty."

She smiled. "Actually there might be a few items you'll enjoy seeing on me. Obviously I didn't pack my sexy stuff for a trip to the ranch."

"Considering how I've reacted to the underwear you already have, I'm not sure my heart can take the racier type."

"We'll do some test runs and see how you hold up. Anyway, knowing my mom, she'll send mostly party dresses to remind me of all I'm giving up." She glanced at him. "Which is nothing, so don't look worried."

"You'll need a party dress for Alex and Tyler's wedding, though."

"I will, won't I? I can hardly wait for them to get back so I can meet them. I like Josie so much that I'm sure I'll like Alex. Morgan keeps saying her sister, Tyler, is way different from her, but still, they're sisters, so I'm sure I'll also like Tyler."

"If Alex loves her, then she has to be great. So did you hear about the best man? Alex's friend from Chicago, the baseball player?"

"I guess not. I've been too focused on the semen expert." She winked at him.

"And I want to keep it that way. Baseball players aren't nearly as sexy as cowboys, right?"

"Right." She laughed. "Unless they're in the major leagues."

"That lets out Logan Carswell, then. He just got dropped by the Cubs. He suffered a career-ending injury of some kind."

"That's too bad."

"It is, but it puts him out of the running for you, which is all to the good." He glanced at Rorschach. "I think the big guy is ready to dismount and meander back to his stall."

"This really feels like a cheat, you know?" She made sure Rorschach climbed down safely and then led him toward the door.

"It's less of a cheat than making love with a condom." He hoisted the canister to his shoulder. "At least these little swimmers have a chance of hitting the big time."

She glanced at him. "Do you think about that much?"

"More, lately."

"This situation between us is getting serious, isn't it?"

He nodded. "'Fraid so."

She met his gaze. "I like that."

His warm smile wrapped her in a cozy blanket of love. "Yeah. Me, too."

* * * * *

COMING NEXT MONTH

Blaze's 10th Anniversary
Special Collectors' Editions

Available July 26, 2011

#627 THE BRADDOCK BOYS: TRAVIS
Love at First Bite
Kimberly Raye

#628 HOTSHOT
Uniformly Hot!
Jo Leigh

#629 UNDENIABLE PLEASURES
The Pleasure Seekers
Tori Carrington

#630 COWBOYS LIKE US
Sons of Chance
Vicki Lewis Thompson

#631 TOO HOT TO TOUCH
Legendary Lovers
Julie Leto

#632 EXTRA INNINGS
Encounters
Debbi Rawlins

HBCNM0711

REQUEST YOUR FREE BOOKS!
2 FREE NOVELS PLUS 2 FREE GIFTS!

red-hot reads!

*Once bitten, twice shy. That's Gabby Wade's motto—
especially when it comes to Adamson men.
And the moment she meets Jon Adamson her theory
is confirmed. But with each encounter a little something
sparks between them, making her wonder if she's been
too hasty to dismiss this one!*

*Enjoy this sneak peek from ONE GOOD REASON
by Sarah Mayberry, available August 2011
from Harlequin® Superromance®.*

Gabby Wade's heartbeat thumped in her ears as she marched to her office. She wanted to pretend it was because of her brisk pace returning from the file room, but she wasn't that good a liar.

Her heart was beating like a tom-tom because Jon Adamson had touched her. In a very male, very possessive way. She could still feel the heat of his big hand burning through the seat of her khakis as he'd steadied her on the ladder.

It had taken every ounce of self-control to tell him to unhand her. What she'd really wanted was to grab him by his shirt and, well, explore all those urges his touch had instantly brought to life.

While she might not like him, she was wise enough to understand that it wasn't always about liking the other person. Sometimes it was about pure animal attraction.

Refusing to think about it, she turned to work. When she'd typed in the wrong figures three times, Gabby admitted she was too tired and too distracted. Time to call it a day.

As she was leaving, she spied Jon at his workbench in the shop. His head was propped on his hand as he studied blueprints. It wasn't until she got closer that she saw his eyes were shut.

He looked oddly boyish. There was something innocent and unguarded in his expression. She felt a weakening in her resistance to him.

"Jon." She put her hand on his shoulder, intending to shake him awake. Instead, it rested there like a caress.

His eyes snapped open.

"You were asleep."

"No, I was, uh, visualizing something on this design." He gestured to the blueprint in front of him then rubbed his eyes.

That gesture dealt a bigger blow to her resistance. She realized it wasn't only animal attraction pulling them together. She took a step backward as if to get away from the knowledge.

She cleared her throat. "I'm heading off now."

He gave her a smile, and she could see his exhaustion.

"Yeah, I should, too." He stood and stretched. The hem of his T-shirt rose as he arched his back and she caught a flash of hard male belly. She looked away, but it was too late. Her mind had committed the image to permanent memory.

And suddenly she knew, for good or bad, she'd never look at Jon the same way again.

Find out what happens next in ONE GOOD REASON, available August 2011 from Harlequin® Superromance®!

Celebrating

Blaze™ **10** *years of*
red-hot reads

Featuring a special August author lineup of
six fan-favorite authors who have written
for Blaze™ from the beginning!

The Original Sexy Six:

Vicki Lewis Thompson
Tori Carrington
Kimberly Raye
Debbi Rawlins
Julie Leto
Jo Leigh

Pick up all six Blaze™
Special Collectors' Edition titles!

August 2011

USA TODAY *bestselling author*

Lynne Graham

introduces her new Epic Duet

THE VOLAKIS VOW

A marriage made of secrets…

Tally Spencer, an ordinary girl with no experience of relationships… Sander Volakis, an impossibly rich and handsome Greek entrepreneur. Sander is expecting to love her and leave her, but for Tally this is love at first sight. Little does he know that Tally is expecting his baby…and blackmailing him to marry her!

PART ONE:
THE MARRIAGE BETRAYAL
Available August 2011

PART TWO:
BRIDE FOR REAL
Available September 2011

Available only from Harlequin Presents®.